TOO MUCH FOR MR. JELLIPOT

Borgo Press Books by S. Fowler Wright

TOO MUCH FOR MR. JELLIPOT

AN INSPECTOR COMBRIDGE AND MR. JELLIPOT CLASSIC CRIME NOVEL

by

S. FOWLER WRIGHT

WRITING AS "SYDNEY FOWLER"

THE BORGO PRESS

An Imprint of Wildside Press LLC

MMIX

CONTENTS

CHAPTER I.

Mr. Quigley Prefers Suicide

"MR. ENOCH QUIGLEY?" Mr. Jellipot repeated. "Yes, show him in."

It was a name which, since he had read the account of the violent end of Phillip Briggs in the *Daily Telegraph* that morning, he had been expecting to hear.

Mr. Quigley was the general manager of the Southern and General Life Assurance Co. Two months before, Mr. Jellipot had been the medium of insuring a client's life with that office for £20,000, and now that client was dead.

Mr. Quigley would be certain to ring him up—or to call.

Now Mr. Quigley came in. He looked worried. He was well-dressed and groomed, as men successful in the insurance world usually are. But he looked flustered now, and uncomfortably hot, though it was a mild day.

He deposited his top hat carefully at the side of the comfortable leather chair into which he sank at the solicitor's invitation. He passed a handkerchief over a bald head as he asked: "I suppose you've heard about Briggs? You know he's dead?"

"I read an account," Mr. Jellipot replied, with his usual precision, "in the *Daily Telegraph* this morning, and I have since had some further details from Inspector Combridge, whom I rang up. On the main fact—that of Mr. Briggs' murder—he confirmed the report."

"Murder? I don't see why he should call it that. The papers only say he was found dead."

"Editors are discreet. Naturally, you would prefer suicide. But I'm afraid there is no doubt."

"A man can cut his own throat."

"Yes. There are some who do. In this case there appears to have been an additional attempt to suffocate him with one of his own pillows."

"I don't gee that that proves anything. He might have tried to hold a pillow down over his own head, and found he hadn't to finish himself to finish himself off that way, and tried something else."

Mr. Jellipot looked surprised at this theory, but he replied politely: "I suppose most things are possible, and some are true which are hard to believe. But there is another difficulty. Mr. Briggs was murdered in his bed, and the weapon—his own razor—with which it was done was found on the dressing table at the other side of the room."

"How do they know he did it with that?"

"They don't. They know that it was used, because, though it was wiped, that was only done superficially. There are traces of blood, both in the hinge and the sheath."

"I don't see that that proves anything either. We've known of men cutting their throats and walking from one room to another afterwards. He might have done it, and then got back into bed."

"And wiped the razor? And left no trace of blood on that side of the room? I am afraid it will be hopeless to ask even a coroner's jury to accept such a theory as that."

"Well, you'd better get us the best counsel you can. We're not going to pay that money without a fight. Not when the first premium hasn't as much as reached our own bank! We thought, coming from you—"

He checked himself, aware that he had gone beyond both reason and courtesy in the implications of this exclamation. But Mr. Jellipot took it quietly, though it was a remark he felt no disposition to overlook.

"I hope," he said, "that you do not suggest that I may have cut a client's throat to bring the insurance money to his estate?"

"No, of course not. We know you too well for that. Besides, what benefit would it be to you? And, by the way, who *does* benefit? That's always an interesting question in such cases."

"Primarily, the creditors of the estate."

"Yes, but beyond that. There'd be a good surplus, with £20,000 thrown into the pool."

"I'm afraid that is more than I am yet able to say."

"But you must have seen that he made a will."

"If he has, it was not drawn by me. In fact, I declined."

Mr. Quigley looked puzzled, and Mr. Jellipot added: "You see, he proposed to leave his estate to me."

Mr. Quigley stared. "I beg your pardon," he said. "Did I understand that—?"

"I think I made myself clear. It was a proposal I did not welcome, and I hope I persuaded him to a more reasonable conclusion. But I believe he went to Redfern & Coote. I am sure that they would give you any information which they properly can. Perhaps, in view of what I have now told you, you would wish that counsel's brief should be drawn by another office than mine?"

"No, of course not, I'm sure you have our entire confidence. Of course, I see—perhaps I ought to consult our chairman. It's a most unusual position." Mr. Quigley got up, looking more flustered than when he had entered the room.

"It is one of those positions," Mr. Jellipot agreed equably, "in which none of us should act with haste. You had better think it over and let me know."

He shook hands with undiminished affability; and, learning next moment that Inspector Combridge was waiting, he said that he would see him at once.

CHAPTER II.

Inspector Combridge Has No Doubt

"I THOUGHT I couldn't do better," Inspector Combridge said, "than to come straight here. I'll say at once that I've come to get information, not to give it. Not that I've got anything to conceal. But there are three men—including Briggs—more or less in the picture who are clients of yours, and I thought you'd tip me off to anything that it may be useful to know. I know I can rely on anything I can get from you, and that's what you can't say about more than one here and there."

"You know the gentleman who must have passed you as he went out?"

"No, I can't say I do."

"He is Mr. Quigley, the general manager of the Southern and General Assurance Co. He would like to hear of an inquest at which a verdict of suicide would be returned."

"Then I can tell him he won't. It's one of the clearest cases of murder I ever saw."

"It would make a difference of £20,000 to his company."

"That's how the land lies, is it? I suppose Briggs had just insured his life, and—"

"He insured it through me, about two months ago, for £20,000. The policy contains the usual clause about suicide. If he kills himself within a year, it is void."

"It looks as though, if we know who benefits by that policy, we mayn't have to look much farther."

"I am not sure that I am not the residuary legatee."

"Then that's one switch-off."

"It is kind of you to say that with such promptitude," Mr. Jellipot smiled. "I must hope that others will take the same view."

"They will, if they're not mugs. But I'm not sure that it goes all the way, even if that's how it is. Who suggested him taking the policy out?"

"Gilson."

"Not Ames?" The inspector looked surprised.

"No. Mr. Gilson not only suggested it, but made it an absolute condition of a substantial investment in Briggs & Co. which he has just made."

"Well, that's another gate banged. Ames might have committed the murder. Of course, that's not saying he did. Gilson couldn't. Not on my present information."

"May I ask why not?"

"He wasn't there."

"Which, in a crime of this character, is surely a conclusive reason. Did the murderer leave any of the usual clues?"

"Not that we've found yet. That's storybook stuff. In real life it's not often they do."

"So I should suppose. It has also occurred to me that the provision of clues of a misleading character must be a simple and elementary precaution that an intelligent murderer might be expected to take. Why should not the trouser button, with its betraying thread, have been taken from his cousin's trousers, instead of his own? Or a pinch of dust from the same turn-ups that could only have been got where his cousin works?"

"Oh, I don't know. I suppose they might. But—"

"Well, we must hope that miscarriages of justice, based on such misleading evidence, do not occur."

"I wouldn't say they don't, now and then. When you once admit a class of evidence that's so easy to fake—but there's nothing of that sort here, bad or good. There's just a dead man, and another headache for us."

"If you would kindly tell me just how the crime was committed, and why you feel so sure that suicide must be ruled out, I might possibly be able to dissuade Quigley from wasting money on a bad brief."

"That's easy. Briggs used to stay in bed till midday. At half past eleven his housekeeper, Mrs. Collis, always took him a cup of cocoa. When she went into the bedroom yesterday morning, she got a shock. There wasn't much to be seen of him—he'd got a pillow more or less over his head—but the bed clothes were in a mess."

"And he was already dead?"

"I should say there's no doubt of that. The murderer must have got hold of his razor first and then put the pillow over his head, and held it down while he cut his throat, which he seems to have clone in such a way that the bed clothes protected him from the blood."

"The use of the pillow may have been merely to prevent him crying out while he could?"

"It was something more than that. The state of the lungs shows considerable asphyxiation, which must have occurred before death. But it wasn't the cause of death. Dr. Mullins is definite about that. The man was still alive when his throat was cut, and that was about as thorough a job as I ever saw."

"You believe the housekeeper?"

"I don't think she did it, if you mean that. She's about five feet high, the wrong side of seventy, and so frail that she leans on the banisters when she goes upstairs. She's still dithering from the shock it gave her when she had her first sight of the bed."

"You said Ames might have done it. What makes you think that?"

"Opportunity. He was in the bedroom from nine-thirty for nearly an hour. It's fair to say that there was nothing unusual in that. He used to go to the works for the letters every morning, and then bring them to Briggs to take his instructions upon them.

"Ames says that was more or less a pretence. He used to leave the real management of the business to him. But that was the way they had."

"In that respect," Mr. Jellipot allowed, "I can confirm the accuracy of what Mr. Ames has said. I have heard of this practice, though it had not dwelt in my mind; and it is a fact that Mr. Briggs was not a good businessman. But it has no doubt occurred to you that the crime, as you have described it, must almost certainly have been committed by someone who was sufficiently familiar with him to enter the bedroom, pick up the razor (presumably knowing where it could be found), and approach the bedside—even seize a pillow—without his suspicions being aroused sufficiently for him to raise an alarm?"

"Which would fit Ames a lot better than most? But it's not as simple as that. Ames says that, when he left, Briggs used to settle off for another doze. It mightn't mean much if he said it alone, but Mrs. Collis says the same thing. She says when she took up the cocoa she often found him asleep."

"And she didn't let anyone in after Ames left?"

"No. She's certain about that. But here again we don't get very far. She's about as deaf as a post, and the front door wasn't locked. Anyone could push it open, and walk in, as, if we let Ames out, we must suppose somebody did."

"As to Ames," Mr. Jellipot said thoughtfully, "I am disposed to think that you must, for which I see more reasons than one.

"In the first place, it would be a most audacious crime, and Ames has impressed me as a particularly circumspect man. It might have been discovered the moment after he left the house, and what possible defence would he have had?

"The second reason is that he had no motive of which I am aware. On the contrary, it was to his interest that Briggs should remain alive. If you are as sure of Gilson as I am of Ames, I think you'll have to look further afield. But you'll understand that better when I've told you what I know of the business relations between these men, which is what I suppose you came here to learn."

CHAPTER III.

WHAT MR. JELLIPOT KNEW

"BRIGGS," Mr. Jellipot said, "has been a client for several years. He was, I believe, of good ability both as a chemist and engineer. He was a successful inventor. But he was not a good businessman.

"He first consulted me in reference to an action regarding one of his patents which might never have been brought had he kept copies of his own letters. As it was, I was fortunate in being able to settle it out of court, at no great expense to him.

"Ames is his business manager. He is a man of some capital of his own, and has consulted me regarding his own investments on some occasions.

"About a year ago, they saw me together. The business, though profitable, was embarrassed through lack of capital, and some creditors were becoming awkward. Ames then lent Briggs £500, on the understanding that it should be repaid within twelve months, when he would require it to meet calls on some shares he held which were not fully paid.

"I was surprised at the time to learn that the business was in that position, for some of Briggs' patents are certainly of great value, but Ames explained at a second interview, when he came alone, that though the management of the business was nominally left to him, Briggs had insisted on a scale of expenditure for advertising, and in other directions, for which only a large capital could provide, even though it should be ultimately profitable. He then said that the sum he had found would be utterly inadequate to meet the position unless there were a radical change of policy, on which he should insist for his own protection.

"About six months ago they saw me again, when Briggs agreed that the financial position had become critical, though he professed bewilderment as to how it had been brought about, and I received the impression that his confidence in Ames—whether in his integrity or his business judgment was not clear—had become shaken.

"I will admit frankly that I had a similar doubt, but the course which Ames had taken, and his attitude to the emergency, were beyond criticism.

"He had advertised, on his own initiative, for someone who would take over the management and introduce additional capital, and he had expressed his willingness to accept a subordinate position, or even to sever his connection with the firm, if that should be a necessary condition of securing the assistance which the business required.

"The advertisement had produced several replies, and it was the negotiations arising from these with which they asked me to deal.

"As to them, I need only say that the applicants withdrew, after becoming informed of a financial position which was sufficiently discouraging, with the exception of Mr. Gilson, who expressed the opinion that the business could be saved by economic and energetic management.

"To make a short tale, he found £2,000 in cash, and arranged for the postponement of substantial liabilities by seeing the creditors individually and giving his personal guarantee of ultimate payment in full.

"But he made one emphatic condition. He said that he regarded Briggs as the most important asset the business had, and he would do nothing unless he entered into a long-term agreement to give his services to the firm, and insured his life for £20,000."

Mr. Jellipot paused, and Inspector Combridge asked: "You saw nothing suspicious in that?"

Mr. Jellipot's reply was unhesitating, though he, perhaps unconsciously, amended the inspector's conventional misuse of an unfortunate word. "I saw nothing to arouse suspicion in that. Certainly not, or I should have declined to act further in the matter. I should have been particularly careful not to—" He checked himself abruptly, aware that he had come near to betraying the confidence of other clients, for his thought had been that he knew too much of the financial condition of the Southern & General to place such a risk with them, had there appeared more than the usual remote possibility of an immediate claim resulting. Not that the Southern & General was unsound. But it had experienced a succession of heavy claims during the current year, which had necessitated the realisation of securities through his office. That was indirectly why the first premium which he had received as their agent had not actually been paid over, for which he might otherwise have sent a special cheque,

15

without waiting to the quarter's end. The last thing they would want would be a further reduction of £20,000 in their Claims Reserve Account before their next Balance Sheet should be issued. He understood how Quigley felt about that. But the doctor's report had been good. Otherwise, even at an increased premium, he would not have advised acceptance of the risk. He brought his mind back to the present issue, as Combridge said: "I can't see anything in what you told me to suggest that either of them would have any quarrel with Briggs, or any motive for killing him. I suppose Ames' position wasn't quite what it had been before?"

"I should say that the difference was not great. Gilson said he didn't want to interfere with the management of the business. He'd got enough to do to attend to his own. He's a stamp dealer in the Strand. He only wanted a financial report, signed by Briggs and Ames, to reach him every week, and if there should be anything in it he didn't like, he'd hare something to say."

"He seems to have shown a singular confidence in the men who, one or both, had got the business into a mess."

"So it appears. But you will remember that the position has only lasted a few weeks. He may have been waiting for them to give him a text on which he could preach his first sermon.

"But he had investigated the business very thoroughly, and it's only fair to Ames to say that he spoke well of him afterwards. His view seems to have been that Ames would be all right, if Briggs didn't interfere on the financial side—Briggs was one of those men who have no sense of the value of money—and he may have felt that he could rely on Ames, knowing he was behind him, to be firm on that. But no doubt you will be seeing Gilson, and what he'll tell you will be better than any guess from me."

"Yes. But it sounds as though I've got to look farther afield, as you said I would."

"So it may be. I suppose that no one, besides the housekeeper, is known to have been in the house when the murder occurred?"

"No. There's a woman who comes in daily for cleaning, but not all the time. She wasn't there till midday yesterday. We can rule her out. And there are two girls—the Misses Reeves—some sort of cousins, who live there more or less. But they were in Cornwall. They'll be back this afternoon. I wonder Briggs didn't leave anything he'd got to them."

"Well, there might be a simple explanation of that," Mr. Jellipot replied, in a tone which suggested that he knew what it was, but he offered no information upon it. The affairs of his clients were not

16

matters for random communication, even to a member of the C.I.D. who was also a trusted friend.

CHAPTER IV.

MR. GILSON'S OPINION

INSPECTOR COMBRIDGE left Mr. Jellipot's office with a feeling that he had made no progress of a positive kind, but without any consequent depression, for he had learnt that the truth is most surely reached by a process of elimination, and that it did not follow that he was on the wrong road because he was not yet in sight of his goal.

"There is one pointer," he thought, "which may alone be sufficient to get me home. The man who wiped that razor, and put it back on the dressing table, didn't want it to appear to be a case of suicide. Perhaps that's also why he tried with the pillow first. It wasn't merely that he didn't try to make it look like suicide, as most murderers would. He went out of his way to make it plain that it couldn't be." There could be only one motive for that—or only one which the inspector could see. He wanted to make it certain that that insurance money would be paid. That ought to narrow the list of suspected persons to two or three…or, perhaps, one. And it would almost certainly preclude occasion to "look farther afield."

But suppose, as Mr. Jellipot had so frankly suggested, that he should prove to be the legatee! It was a position at which even Inspector Combridge, who was not disposed to take his work mirthfully, was obliged to smile. And yet, if, under some fantastic combination of circumstances, Mr. Jellipot had felt that the elimination of the inventor would be for the benefit of mankind? Would he hesitate on moral grounds? Or for fear of the law? It was a baffling proposition. The only certainty was that such a murder would not be crudely committed, and it was improbable that it would be easy—perhaps even that it would be possible—to prove. It was professional caution rather than friendly feeling that prompted the half-articulate exclamation: "Heaven save us from that!"

While engaged in these reflections, from leaving Mr. Jellipot's Basinghall Street offices, the inspector had reached Cheapside. Now he thought: "I'll take Gilson next, and see what I can make of him." He mounted a bus for the Strand.

Mr. Gilson's office was on the top floor. It was in a large suite of offices to which there was more than one entrance from the street. Its corridors were badly lit. Their doors needed paint. They were not very well cleaned. The whole effect was depressing—faintly sinister to one sensitive to atmosphere, or to whom, like Inspector Combridge, suspicion was an attitude of mind which it was his constant duty to maintain.

But the occupation of sordid offices in the Strand is no evidence of having committed a murder in Antrobus Road, N.12, and Mr. Gilson's office itself was neat, clean, and in every way consistent with the business which he professed to follow.

There was a small anteroom crossed by a polished counter, on which was an electric bell-push with the words *Please ring* in a semi-circle of bright metal letters beneath it. There was no sign of any staff, but when Inspector Combridge touched the bell Mr. Gilson appeared at the inner door, heard his name without any exhibition of surprise or other emotion, said: "I suppose it's something about this tragedy at Antrobus Road," and lifted the flap of the counter.

Inspector Combridge was invited in to a larger room, in the centre of which was a large flat desk, almost entirely clear of papers or other articles, except a large inkstand, and a microscope which he recognized as being of a particularly expensive make. Before the stamp dealer's chair there was a blotting pad on which lay a sheet of white paper, and on it a blue stamp which appeared to have suffered somewhat from dirt and age.

Inspector Combridge, being seated on the opposite side of the desk, was subconsciously aware that numerous cabinets containing shallow drawers stood round the walls, with a large cupboard at the farther end; but his mind was upon the man before him—a man suave of voice, mild of manner, and who appeared to be entirely at ease, and free from fear that suspicion of having committed a frightful crime might be hovering at his own door. Yet his first words showed that the idea had, at least, been brought before him, even if it had assumed no serious aspect.

"I must tell you at once that I know nothing of the murder (of which I first heard in this morning's papers), and it is very improbable that I can be of any important assistance to your investigations; but I should add—of which you might otherwise not be informed—

19

that I was in Antrobus Road yesterday morning at about ten-thirty, and should probably have called upon Mr. Briggs had I not been already a few minutes late for an appointment in Buckhurst Road."

Inspector Combridge concealed any surprise he may have felt at this statement. He replied: "You actually passed the house at that time? You did not observe anyone leaving it? Or anything else of a suspicious character?"

Mr. Gilson, however expert and precise he may have been in his knowledge of foreign stamps, evidently lacked Mr. Jellipot's precision of speech. He answered what the Inspector had evidently intended to ask, without appearing conscious that he had not done so.

"No, I can't say I did. I met Mr. Ames, but there was nothing out of the way in that. I believe he went there more mornings than not."

"You spoke to him?"

"Just a few words. I asked how the business was getting on. I might have said more, but I was in a hurry. I am particular about keeping appointments punctually, and I was already a few minutes late."

"You noticed nothing unusual in his manner?"

"No. I can't say I did. Not as though he'd just cut somebody's throat, if you mean that. And, besides, what reason could he have? They got on well enough together, as far as I ever saw. But there was something this morning I didn't like, and I made up my mind I should tell you I'd been past the door, even if I had to ring you up to do it."

Mr. Gilson paused a moment, as though hesitating over his next words, and Inspector Combridge encouraged him mendaciously with the assurance that it's always best to be frank with the police—always best in the end.

"Ames rang me up this morning to ask several questions as to now the business is to be carried on—about signing cheques, for one thing—all natural questions that he was bound to be bothering about, but he mentioned having seen me near the house in a way that I didn't like, and I wasn't going to have him making anything out of that."

"You mean you thought he might mention it to us, and you'd naturally prefer that we should hear it from you?"

"No. It was the other way round. He brought it up to assure me that he'd be particular not to mention it to you. I disliked the implications of that, and I had no intention of putting myself into a position where I could be blackmailed by him."

"You mean he threatened that?"

"No. That would be going too far. He just hinted that he would be doing me a favour by keeping his mouth shut, and it was one that I preferred not to accept."

"I see. There would be a good deal less blackmail going on if everyone had the wisdom to act in the same way. You will understand that it is a matter of form, and that you are under no obligation to answer, when I ask you if you care to let me know what business took you in that direction?"

"No. There's no secret about that. I had an appointment with a man in Smith's Terrace for ten-thirty to inspect a stamp collection he wants to sell. It's an experience we often have with private collectors. They don't like their stamps to go out of their own sight. I don't blame them for that. There might be abstractions or substitutions that can't be proved."

"Did you buy the collection?"

"No. I was there more than an hour examining it, and haggling over the price. The trouble was that he'd no idea of the value himself, and whatever I'd offered, he'd have been afraid to accept."

"I suppose there really is a rather wide margin between what you sell at, and what you give?"

"Yes. There may be," Mr. Gilson answered frankly. "But it's not as simple as that. Values are all unreal, and they change abruptly. Then, really rare stamps go out of fashion, and you can't sell them at all. It isn't so much that the price drops as that there's no market at all. You just have to wait for them to come back. If there are enough dealers interested, you can make a market again, sooner or later. If there aren't, you're sunk, more likely than not. It's a queer business."

Having got on to the topic that so largely engaged his mind, Mr. Gilson went on, and the inspector let him talk. He felt that he was learning his man, as it was his business to do. "Now, this stamp I was examining when you came in—if it's a forgery, it's one of the best that I ever saw. If it's not—well, you can judge for yourself. It comes to me in a parcel of nearly two thousand, which the owner says he's willing to sell for ten pounds. He says he knows what they are worth, and that he won't take a penny less. Now, except this one, the total value to me is about fifteen shillings. They'd mostly go in packets at twenty shillings the thousand, and I'd have to give a big discount on that—or have advertising expenses, which comes to the same thing. But this stamp is a forgery, or worth nearly two hundred pounds."

"And you can't be sure?"

"No. And there aren't many men in the trade who would. I should have passed it as genuine without much hesitation if it had come to me in a different way. But, you see, if it's a forgery, there'll be a lot like it to be got on to the market one way or other, and this is one that's likely to be tried. If I send the packet back, they post it to another dealer, and if I buy it, and then find that the stamp's a forgery, I've got no remedy. The man professes ignorance. And I'm in the position of having tried to get his valuable stamp (for I must have thought it genuine when I bought the parcel) for a tithe of its true value. So, of course, anyone in our business would, if he got the chance; but, all the same, it doesn't tend to promote sympathy for us if we get one in the eye."

"It is evidently," the inspector agreed, "a difficult business; and one which must need a great deal of expert knowledge. I suppose you have been in it for many years?"

"Well, I opened up here about six years ago. I'd been collecting since I was six, and specialised in British Colonies. Some of the stamps that I paid coppers for when I was a boy had become worth enough to give me a good start. And my income tax returns show that I haven't done badly since."

Inspector Combridge agreed as to the conclusive nature of that evidence. There may be a man who, from vanity, or some more exceptional motive, falsely returns profits he does not make, and so renders himself liable to the heavy penalties that are provided for deliberate inaccuracy in such documents, but he would not be easy to find. He brought the conversation back to its immediate subject by asking: "You don't mind giving me the name of the man in Smith's Terrace?"

"No. Not at all. I hope you'll find time to look him up."

"Yes. I shall do that. It is in the interest of all who come in contact, however remotely, with a crime of this kind, that their innocence should be established by full enquiry, and it is often the only way by which the criminal can be discovered with certainty. I wish everyone took it as sensibly as you evidently do."

"Well," Mr. Gilson replied reasonably, "it seems obvious. Someone's done it, and we're all strangers to you."

"Apart from giving me this information regarding your own movements, do you think you can tell me anything which might throw light on the perpetrator of the crime?"

Mr. Gilson did not immediately answer. He looked thoughtful. He said, after a pause which the inspector was too experienced to interrupt: "Of course, I see what you're asking me. You want to know whether I know of any motive Ames might have had? And, in short, do I think it was he?

"Well, I don't like Ames. I think he's deep. If I say crafty, it mightn't be too strong a word. But that's just a feeling. I'm speaking frankly, knowing that you'll take it as confidential. I don't think he's one who'd do such a thing in a fit of temper. He'd need to have a strong motive—a very strong one, I should suggest. And it isn't easy to see what it could be."

"Yes," the inspector replied thoughtfully, "I should say you've summed him up about right, and I'm much obliged to you for being so frank."

He had already seen Mr. Ames, and while he had felt no inclination to trust him, his expressions of concern, which had been directed more to how the death of one of his employers would affect himself, than to any regret for the dead man, had impressed him as genuine of their kind.

He shook hands with Mr. Gilson in a friendly manner, and it was only as he regained the street that it occurred to him that the innocence of the stamp dealer was still something less than proved.

He had seemed to be less interested in the murder than in the authenticity of a dubious stamp. That might be a deliberate pose. Or it might be the callousness of a criminal mind. But the inspector thought not. Besides, what motive could Gilson have? To get the business more entirely under his own control? It seemed inadequate. All the same, the alibi he had offered must be most carefully probed.

But the probability appeared to be that the crime was not the work of either of the business associates of the dead man.

He must enquire as to his private life, and any possible enmities it might include. He hoped the Misses Reeves could help him in that. He had already made an appointment to see them that evening. And Mrs. Collis might be sufficiently recovered to answer questions more coherently than she had yet done. There was no need to despair.

CHAPTER V.

AN INTERVIEW WITH TWO GIRLS

BEFORE keeping his evening appointment, Inspector Combridge went back to Scotland Yard, to report to Superintendent Roomer the result of the enquiries he had already made, and to compare opinions upon them.

The superintendent did not believe in magnifying difficulties, or giving praise for good work with a liberal tongue. His own promotion had been due to a long course of undistinguished service, in which he may have been fortunate in avoiding error rather than in any outstanding achievement, until he had been entrusted with the elucidation of the great diamond robbery at Devizes, in which he had shown either dazzling genius, or enjoyed luck of almost supernatural quality. The opinion of his brother officers had no hesitation in choosing between these alternatives, but they recognized the inevitability of the promotion which followed. And, after all, was it not luck on which they must all largely depend at last?

"You ought to find this a simple case," he had said, as he assigned Combridge to the investigation, and the inspector, who knew that he was now on the threshold of a promotion which only some egregious blunder could delay much longer, sincerely hoped that he might be right.

Now the superintendent listened to his report without the indiscretion of expressing any decided opinion, unless it were when he commented on the insurance policy: "There may be more than meets the eye there. You'd better see Redfern & Coote first thing in the morning, and find out how the land lies. With these slimy lawyers, you never quite know where you are."

Inspector Combridge ventured the opinion that the adjective could not be applied appropriately to Mr. Jellipot, and the superintendent said: "Perhaps not, but you never know. Why should Briggs be leaving money to him? Can you tell me that?" And Inspector Combridge must admit that it was beyond his power to do so.

The superintendent shifted his ground. "You've eliminated robbery as the motive?"

"As the motive, it seems unlikely. I don't think we can go farther than that.

"We couldn't prove that anything was stolen at all. A signet ring of some value Briggs used to wear was left on the dressing table untouched, and must have been seen, for the razor was laid down only about six inches away.

"But there was no money in the wallet in the breast pocket of his coat, which hung over the back of a chair by the bed, and Mrs. Collis says that he always had a good supply there.

"Ames confirmed that without hesitation. He says he used to take him ten pounds in cash every Monday, and when he put it away there would usually be a good bit there already. He reckons that Briggs usually had from twenty to thirty in cash in that wallet."

"You don't suppose Ames would murder him to get hold of such an amount?"

"No. It isn't sense. Though there are plenty who would. But he might have taken it to make it look like motive, though that's a long way from saying he did. But I'd say someone did, more likely than not. It isn't the kind of murder that's committed to steal cash from a wallet."

"You may know a bit more when you've seen those young women tonight."

This being indisputable, Inspector Combridge merely gave such assent as politeness to a superior officer will require, and left to interview the young women of whom they spoke.

The Misses Reeves were alike in being young and attractive girls, and of a style and manner such as the inspector had not expected to see. But when that has been said, similarities are at an end, and differences begin.

The elder, Muriel, was evidently in a frightened, which might easily have developed into a hysterical, state. There was, to the inspector, nothing surprising in that. It is a disturbing incident to be brought back suddenly from Cornwall by the news that your uncle's throat had been most efficiently cut, and there are many women who are nervously disturbed by a visit from the police on more trivial occasions.

But the younger girl, Belle, seemed as cool as her summer frock, and to treat the murder, not indeed with levity, but without emotion or any visible disturbance of mind.

He was introduced to them by the housekeeper, who was formal, in her rather quavering voice, to distinguish: "Miss Reeves, Miss Arabella Reeves," or he might have concluded that Muriel was the younger sister.

Belle opened the conversation. "You want to see us about Uncle's death?" Her brown eyes regarded him with a cool gravity. It was as though he were under examination, rather than the instrument of the probing law. Or, at least, as though he were expected to explain why this murder had not been averted, and why the murderer was still at large. And these young women had kept him waiting for over half an hour, on the pretext that they had only just come in, and must have a meal!

He knew the hour of arrival of the Cornish express, and thought that he had allowed them ample time for that. With this uppermost in his mind, he replied: "I thought you would have got back sooner."

He thought that Muriel looked frightened at this remark. Did she suppose that she might be in danger of some legal penalty, if it could be shown that she had not returned with the utmost haste? She was not unlike her younger sister, but her hair was duller in colour and less abundant than Belle's heavy chestnut waves, and her brown eyes were less brilliant, and less direct. Now she began, in a voice of apology: "We should have—" and was silenced by Belle's curter and more assured reply: "Well, we didn't. But we'd like to hear what you can tell us now."

"I hoped that I might have been able to get some useful information from you."

"I don't know why you should. It isn't likely when we weren't here."

This was not rudely said. It was with a smile, and Belle's smiles were pleasant to see. But it still held the implication that it was the inspector's part to defend and explain. Her holiday (if such it were) had been interrupted, and it was reasonable to ask how such an event could have been allowed to occur, and to have assurances that it was being efficiently dealt with now.

No detective will rise high in the ranks of criminal investigators if he allow irritation to rule his words. Inspector Combridge was practised in self-restraint. But there was an emphatic curtness in his reply: "Your uncle has been murdered, we do not yet know by whom. It is natural to ask you if you can give us information which will assist us in finding the criminal."

"It was Mr. Ames, of course. I should have thought you would see that."

Muriel's weak interposition: "Oh, Belle, I don't think you should say that," went unregarded as Combridge asked:

"Will you tell me why you are so sure?"

"Because he was with Uncle, and then Uncle was dead."

"You think it is as simple as that? Have you any other reason to think that Mr. Ames might have murdered your uncle?"

"Mr. Ames might murder anybody. Muriel, isn't he just the sort?"

Muriel looked worried, and more frightened than before. She repeated: "Belle, I don't think you ought to say that."

"Why not, if I'm asked? The policeman asked what I thought, and he knows now. You know I say what I think, more times than not."

"Well," Inspector Combridge said, "I'm not objecting to that. I am glad to have your opinion so frankly expressed. But, you know, opinions don't go very far in a court of law. What we need is proof."

"And you can't expect us to give you that when we weren't there."

"No. But you might be able to give me facts which would assist me in the right direction."

"Might we? I don't see how. But if it's too much for the police, I suppose we shall have to take it up, sooner or later. I don't see why he should kill Uncle Adrian and get away with it, as you seem to think he might."

"Really, Miss Arabella, I didn't say that. I expressed no opinion as to who the culprit may be, and I certainly didn't suggest that he will escape the penalty of his crime."

"No, you didn't. And if I may say it without sounding rude, I didn't suggest you did."

The reply was less curt than its record sounds, the girl's smile, and pleasantly inflected speech, taking the edge from incisive words.

Undiscouraged, Inspector Combridge, true to his reputation for pertinacious pursuit rather than any brilliance of intuition, tried another line of approach. "I suppose," he asked, "you have lived with your uncle a long time? You were more or less familiar with his affairs?"

"Oh, we don't live here! Only when we're in London, that is."

"Which is a large part of the year?"

"Sometimes more, sometimes less. It's been six months before now."

"And this has been going on for a long time?"

"Since Mother died three years ago."

"And your father is not alive either?"

"No. He died before that."

"And when you are not here?"

"We are with another uncle in Cornwall—Sir Phillip Reeves. We reckon that's our home more than this."

"I see. But you like to be in London a good deal of the time? May I conclude that your parents left you with means of your own?"

"Really, inspector, I don't see what that has to do with you!"

"No. Perhaps not. Though we like a clear background. But you haven't answered the more important question I asked—how far you may have been familiar with your uncle's affairs?"

"You mean about the business muddles, and about Mr. Gilson coming in? We knew about as much as he did himself. He talked it all over with us. But I wouldn't say it was clear to him."

"You mean he wasn't a good businessman?"

"He didn't understand much about money, if you mean that. He was always easy to cheat."

"You mean he may have been cheated?"

"By Mr. Ames? I'd have called it a safe guess. But Mr. Gilson said not. He said he'd trust the business with Mr. Ames, if Uncle would leave it alone, except the inventing part."

Inspector Combridge considered this, and a suspicion arose which had not entered his mind previously. "You don't think that Mr. Ames had met Mr. Gilson previously—before he answered the advertisement?"

Arabella looked surprised at the suggestion. "No. It wouldn't be likely, would it? They weren't friends, if you mean that. Mr. Gilson said Mr. Ames was all right, but Mr. Ames didn't like Mr. Gilson."

"Although he introduced him—or, at least, got him through his own advertisement? Well, that's possible. He may have been jealous of a new man coming in. But that's no reason why he should kill your uncle."

"No. It couldn't have been that."

Muriel's timid voice interposed: "Belle, I think you ought to tell the inspector they wouldn't meet."

"Yes. We did think that was queer! Uncle tried to get them together here, but they never would."

"You mean that Ames and Gilson wouldn't meet? But I should have thought—"

"Oh, they must have met often enough! I didn't mean that. But not here. They must have met at the works."

"But they didn't meet your uncle together? What excuse did they make for that?"

Muriel interposed again: "It isn't right to say they. It was Mr. Ames. Mr. Gilson came both times."

"I see," the inspector said, being by no means sure that he did. Vaguely, the information prejudiced him against the too-absent Ames, though its implications were hard to specify. Anyway, he saw that it was evidence offered in a spirit of hostility. The young ladies regarded the business manager without liking or trust. That might be the reputed intuition of women, or it might be no more than a reflection of their uncle's feeling—the unreasonable irritation of a man who sought to blame his manager for his own faults. But it seemed likely that, if these two young women were left to talk the matter over further between themselves—and perhaps with the house-keeper, who would doubtless speak more freely to them than she could be persuaded to do to the police—there might be more to be learned than there was now. The inspector got up to go.

"I don't think I'll worry you any more tonight," he said. "When you've thought things over, something else may occur to you that I ought to know. It's right to be suspicious of everyone till we get at the truth, but I wouldn't talk as though you are sure that Mr. Ames did it. Not on anything that we know yet."

But though he warned them thus, he was conscious of a strengthening conviction, against which he must warn himself of the necessity for keeping an open mind. And, if it *were* Ames, what on earth could the motive be?

Well, there was that alibi of Gilson's to be investigated. It was no use trying to add up a column before all the figures were there. It was not more than five minutes walk to Buckhurst Road. He would do it now.

CHAPTER VI.

An Unintended Surprise

SMITH'S Terrace, a cul-de-sac on the east side of Buckhurst Road, about halfway up, is of a quiet respectability suitable to that of the elderly stamp collector who himself opened the door of his single-fronted, semi-detached residence, and received the inspector with a rather nervous affectation of cordiality, which concealed a lively, and perhaps apprehensive, curiosity as to what his business could be.

He led the way into a back living room, made cheerful by a glow of fire in the grate, though the weather was not cold. There was a table in the middle of the room with writing materials scattered upon it. It was clear that Mr. Blake had been dealing with his correspondence, sitting with his back to the fire.

He turned his chair round, and invited Inspector Combridge to take a more comfortable one at the side of the hearth. As the inspector passed the table, he noticed that one letter lay sealed and stamped, and that it was addressed to Gilson & Co., Stamp Dealers, Strand, W.C.2. It confirmed, to some extent, the truth of Gilson's statement. But what might that envelope contain, which could scarcely have been meant for him to see?

Anyway, it made a direct opening for the enquiry on which he came. "I can't help seeing," he said, "that you've got a letter to Gilson & Co. ready to post. It was really about that that I came. Am I correct in thinking that Mr. Gilson has seen you recently?"

"Yes," was the ready answer, Mr. Blake showing some relief of manner now that he knew the subject of the call, or, at least, that it appeared to be one in which he would have no direct concern. "He was here yesterday morning. I hope there hasn't been any accident?"

"No. But there was a murder in Antrobus Road. I expect you'll have heard of that? There's nothing against Mr. Gilson, but it's rather important to time everything that happened. Could you tell me—I want you to be as careful as you possibly can—what time he called yesterday, and how long he stayed?"

"Yes. I can tell you that. Or, at least, what time he came. That clock there struck the quarter—a quarter to eleven it was—just as I heard the bell and got up to let him in. I always keep it five minutes fast, so that makes it twenty to."

"Was that the time you were expecting him?"

"No. He was to have been here at ten-thirty. He was ten minutes late. He mentioned that he'd been hindered for a few minutes talking to someone he met. But I told him it didn't make any difference to me."

"He made a point of telling you that he'd met someone?"

"He just mentioned it."

"And about how long did he stay?"

"Oh, a good while. It couldn't have been much less than an hour, but I didn't notice particularly. Not the time when he went."

"You probably knew Mr. Gilson before yesterday?"

"I've done business with him—buying, not selling. I hadn't seen him before. It had been done by post."

"Satisfactory business, I've no doubt?"

"Yes. I'd no complaint, or I shouldn't have gone to him now. He's always kept his prices up, but he doesn't send out poor quality specimens, and that's what collectors like."

"I expect there'll be correspondence showing how the appointment was made?"

"No. It was on the phone. Last Monday. I rang him up and said I'd got a good selection to sell, and would he care to give me a call."

"You sell as well as buy?"

"I haven't done much till now. But I'm giving up. I'm selling the lot."

"But you didn't make a deal?"

"Not yesterday. He offered me a price I wouldn't take. But I've altered my mind since. As a matter of fact, that letter's to say he can have them."

Mr. Blake picked up the letter in a hesitant hand. He looked at the inspector as though querying that which he would not put into words. Inspector Combridge felt that justice required that the doubt should not remain. Ames, on his own statement, had left Briggs' house at about half-past ten. Gilson had been here about ten minutes later. It would be absurd to suppose that he had crept into the house in Antrobus Road during those brief minutes, engaged his victim's attention in such a way that he could approach him without rousing suspicion, cut his throat, and then come along here, calm and ready

31

for the inspection of stamps—no, it would not do. He said: "I hope you understand that my enquiry does not imply anything whatever against Mr. Gilson. What you have told me confirms what we have already heard. It was just routine work checking it up."

Mr. Blake said he was pleased to hear that, and then added: "But I was sorry to hear of Mr. Briggs' death. I hope you get the devil who did it. He was too good to come to an end like that."

"You speak as though you knew him."

"So I did. Just to speak to, not more. He used to go to the same chapel on Sunday evenings. I've heard say he wouldn't get up early enough for the morning service."

Inspector Combridge rose to go. It did not seem that there was likely to be much profit from discussing so slight an acquaintance. And by doing so he almost missed that which he was to be startled to hear.

"I'm sorry," Blake went on, "for the two young ladies. It must have been a shock to them."

"Yes, I'm afraid it was." The tone was casual. They were in the passage now.

"Pretty girls they are, too. Especially the younger. I saw her only last Monday—"

Inspector Combridge woke up. "Last Monday? That's scarcely possible. They only came back from Cornwall this afternoon."

But Mr. Blake, without appearing to take much interest in the matter, was unshaken in his reply: "You must be wrong about that. She was in Portman's on Monday."

"You're quite sure?"

Mr. Blake said he was. He revealed that he was the head waiter at Portman's. Did the Misses Reeves know him? No, how should they? Except they might know him by sight, as the head waiter there.

But, anyway, he knew them. The younger in particular. She always did the ordering. Rather difficult to please, but she tipped well.

Inspector Combridge thought he would have something to say to those young women at their next meeting. It might have nothing to do with the murder—it was not easy to see how it could—but he disliked being deceived. And anything that is mysterious in the environment of such a crime is a matter to be followed up till the truth be bare.

CHAPTER VII.

WHY THERE WAS NO WILL

MR. COOTE was a small suave man with a frankness of manner which gave an effect of candour to measured words.

He greeted Inspector Combridge as though he were a client of opulent purse and litigious dispositions.

"You have come, I have no doubt," he said, "in reference to this sad tragedy at Antrobus Road."

"Yes. I understand that Mr. Jellipot recommended Briggs to you for the drawing up of a will which he was not disposed to deal with himself."

"That was the position. Mr. Briggs proposed to make him his residuary legatee, and he naturally objected to act, in view of that circumstance."

"I suppose professional etiquette—"

"There is no prohibition. But most solicitors would agree that it would have been unwise. The natural heirs—there are two nieces, as you will know—might have alleged undue influence, or raised other difficulties."

"It seems a bit odd that Briggs should have overlooked them."

"Yes? Perhaps it does. But he told me that they are well provided for already. Their father was an exceptionally rich man. He may also have been influenced by a feeling—possibly quite groundless—that they preferred the home of their paternal uncle, and only made a convenience of him."

"You don't mean that he was on bad terms with them?"

"Not at all. He spoke of them with affection. But he didn't consider that they needed any money from him."

"All the same, it isn't quite usual for a man to leave everything to his solicitor."

"No. It certainly isn't, or most of us would be better off than we are. But I believe Briggs had a particular esteem for Mr. Jellipot,

33

and a sense of gratitude which is also less general than we might like it to be. The trouble was that Jellipot didn't welcome the idea. In fact, he expressed himself on the telephone, when he first spoke to me about it, with exceptional vigour. He said he was a single man, making more money than he found occasion to spend, and if we couldn't persuade Briggs to change his mind, it would probably end in his refusing to accept the benefaction."

"And Briggs made the will although he must have known how Mr. Jellipot felt?"

"Actually, there is no will."

"I thought you said—"

"I think not. We have been discussing a position which had not fully developed. The fact is that we advised Briggs that, if the benefaction should be refused, the will might become void unless an alternative should be provided.

"After some reflection, he instructed us that, if Mr. Jellipot should feel himself unable to accept his liberality, or if he should predecease him (which was not improbable, for he was the older man), the money should be left to the business."

"I don't quite understand that. The business was Gilson and himself. You mean it was to be left to Gilson?"

"Not precisely, though the benefit would have been his. It was to be expended in specific ways in the development of some of his patented articles, in which Gilson's interest might be less than his own. You will appreciate that Briggs was more interested in his own ideas than in the profit which they might ultimately bring.

"There are legal difficulties in the wording of such a provision which I need not explain in detail, but we did our best with it, and sent the draft will for his approval.

"That was three weeks ago. It could have been engrossed and signed in forty-eight hours, but he objected that he had not made his meaning clear. He insisted on a wording we could not approve, and in the end it was agreed that we should take counsel's opinion upon it. That opinion reached us yesterday afternoon."

"So he actually died intestate?"

"I have no doubt that that is the position."

"And the Misses Reeves will inherit his property—which is, more or less, the insurance money—which they would have lost if the will had been executed?"

"The money will go to his legal heirs."

"That is saying much the same thing."

"So I should suppose. But you surely would not suggest that they would have instigated the murder for such a motive?"

"No. I should call it highly improbable, even absurd. Though we do come up against some queer things where large sums of money are involved. But I am just trying to get at what the facts were. Should you say that Gilson and Ames knew of the provisions of the proposed will—or that it had not been executed?"

"Ames certainly knew of the provisions. I can't say anything about Gilson. I suppose not. As to whether they had any reason to conclude that it had, or had not, been executed, I know nothing at all."

"If they thought it had, the murder might be of advantage to them?"

"Well, you have the facts. You can judge that as well as I. I know you attach great importance to motive in investigating crimes of this character, but if you rely on that, you might say that Jellipot—if he supposed the will to have been executed—had the greatest motive of all, or the Misses Reeves, if they thought it hadn't, but soon would be. And any of them more than Gilson or Ames. There are only the small points on the other side that they're not the sort of people to do it, and that they weren't there."

"No. But we don't go on motive alone. It's just a weight in the scale. And it needs a lot else to weight the scale down if it isn't there also. Well, I'm much obliged to you. I don't get the picture yet, but the pieces are falling into shape, one by one."

The inspector shook hands, and left. And then, because it was only two minutes walk to Mr. Jellipot's office, and it was too late to do much else before lunch, he looked in there, and found the solicitor disengaged.

"I thought," he said, "that you'd be interested to know that the will wasn't executed." He went on to narrate what he had learned, and Mr. Jellipot listened quietly.

"Personally," he said, "I am glad to know that the question of a will does not arise. But it leaves it an even more intricate problem than it was previously."

"Which is as good as saying that the murderer was whoever thought the insurance money would come to him?"

"To him or her, or perhaps them," Mr. Jellipot amended, with his usual particularity.

"You mean the girls might be in it?"

"It is theoretically possible. It does not follow that it would be a sensible theory."

"Would you say either of those girls could tell a good lie?"

"I have observed that the number of people who will lie on what they consider sufficient occasion (as to which there may be profound differences of opinion) is not small. I suppose they could. I would hazard the opinion that the younger would tell a good one, if she told any at all."

"They were supposed to be in Cornwall when the crime was committed, and to have come back yesterday afternoon."

"So you told me. I know nothing beyond that."

"That's what Mrs. Collis told me. She said she'd wired for them to come back, and I saw the reply. It looked genuine to me. But they weren't there. The younger one was seen in London last Monday."

"That is also interesting, but it is a large assumption that it is any business of the police."

"Oh, we'll make it our business! We've no use for lying in such matters as these. But," the inspector exclaimed, with a sudden change of tone, "I believe you've got a theory of what happened, and don't take much account of what doesn't fit in with that."

"I have," Mr. Jellipot admitted, "had an idea, but it's not one I should care to mention, because it's almost certainly wrong. And if it should be wrong, I should lay myself open to more ridicule than, I admit frankly, I should choose to incur.

"But, if I should be right, it's a matter which the inquest will almost certainly bring to light. Because, if it be true, certain things will almost certainly happen, and, if those things happen, it will be almost certainly true."

Inspector Combridge frowned over this statement, and there was no gratitude in his voice as he replied: "That sounds all right, but as there won't be any inquest—"

"No inquest? I am surprised. I should have thought—"

"So should I. But it's not one of those matters that I decide. The Assistant-Commissioner thinks it's a clear case. I expect he'll be asking why I haven't arrested Ames before he goes home tonight. But I'm not sure, and if I make a mistake there'll be all the kicks for me. The coroner's just going to take formal evidence tomorrow, and adjourn *sine die*, if we haven't made any arrest by then. I think I'll see Ames again. I daresay you're right that if I go after the girls I shall be barking under the wrong tree." With these words, very moodily said, the inspector got up to go.

CHAPTER VIII.

WHAT MRS. FISHWICK SAW

INSPECTOR COMBRIDGE did not see Ames in the afternoon. He looked in at Scotland Yard, and found a message waiting there which turned his thoughts to another track. There was a Mrs. Fishwick living in Antrobus Road who had information to give. He went there at once.

Mrs. Fishwick lived in a first-floor room almost opposite to the house in which the tragedy had occurred. It was a room which she did not leave.

She had been wealthy once, but her husband had been ruined (she said) through trusting a false-hearted friend.

Having been ruined, he promptly died, leaving poverty and regrets to her.

She did not read the newspapers now. She read the Bible, concentrating on the cursing psalms. *Vengeance is mine, I will repay, saith the Lord*. What could be more satisfactory than that?

When she raised her eyes from the portions of Hebrew scripture to which her mind responded, she would watch the quiet road, until there would be little of the exterior movements of her immediate neighbours, and those who visited them, that she did not know.

She had been silently intrigued by the evidences of some exciting disturbance at No. 48, but it had not been her custom to encourage conversation with those who waited upon her. The separating distance was too great. But on the second day, when the usual morning caller did not mount No. 48's three front-door steps, curiosity triumphed, and she heard much from a voluble maid, including efforts of local imagination on which it is needless to dwell, as they went wide both of the facts and what the police at this stage supposed them to be. But their result was to decide Mrs. Fishwick that it was her duty to disclose what she had seen.

She did not rise when Inspector Combridge entered her room, nor was she quick to invite him to take a chair. She remembered a village constable, who had been her cook's nephew, whom the idea of sitting in her presence would have reduced to a red-faced confusion. Inspector Combridge did not resent this attitude. He would have stood, not merely on his feet but his head, if he could have advanced the enquiry on which he was engaged by that posture. But there came a time during the subsequent conversation when he sat down, and the lady did not appear to observe the uninvited liberty.

"You are Mrs. Fishwick?" he began. "I understand you can give us some information bearing on the death of Mr. Briggs at Number Forty-Eight, on the other side of the road."

"I didn't ask them to tell you that. I said I could tell you who went in and out of the house the morning before last, if that's when it happened."

"That is what we should very much like to know."

"There was the gentleman who used to call, more mornings than not, at about half-past nine. A rather short man, rather stout, and always looking untidy, as though he didn't know how to brush his clothes."

"That would be Mr. Ames."

"I don't know his name. He usually came out about a quarter-past ten. Sometimes earlier. He didn't come out till half-past ten that morning."

"There was nothing very uncommon in that?"

"No. I've known him later. But he was earlier most mornings."

"Did he appear to be in any particular hurry?"

"No. Not specially. He was often rather in a bustle when he came out."

"And after that?"

"There was a young man who'd been once or twice before. He called about five minutes after the other gentleman left."

"He went in?"

"Yes. He stayed about ten minutes. Not more than that."

"Did you see who let him in?"

"Yes. The old woman who always opens the door."

"And was there anyone after that?"

"No. Not at the front. The butcher called a bit later, but he went round to the back."

"And of course he was there long?"

"No. He was back almost at once."

"Well, I'm much obliged to you. Should you know the young man, if you should see him again?"

"Yes, I think I might. He was quite young, rather tall, and fair-haired. He didn't wear a hat."

"Well, I'm much obliged to you for the help you've given." He got up to go.

He saw that, if this witness could be believed, the crime was almost certainly committed by Ames. The only others who could possibly have done it were the hatless youth, the butcher, and Mrs. Collis.

The young man must have done his work with astonishing celerity, if it were he; and the butcher with an even greater expedition (though it was certainly in his line!). But that must have been by arrangement with Mrs. Collis, which was absurd. It is not an English custom to ask the butcher to slaughter one of the family when he calls with the morning's meat.

Mrs. Collis must be acquitted on other grounds. She was not physically fit for the job. But she must have lied to him when she said she had had no other callers. That made two. Why did women lie so often on non-essential points in these cases, causing so much needless trouble to the police? Well, he supposed their reasons seemed good to them!

He paused a moment to ask: "I suppose you weren't looking out all the time? Someone might easily have called whom you didn't see?"

"No. I was looking out till lunch came. That was at a quarter to one. And the rumpus started before then. Till your car came, there couldn't have been anyone calling I didn't see. I believe that's the same young man coming along now. Yes, he's calling at the house."

"So he certainly is." With little ceremony of leave-taking, Inspector Combridge ran down the stairs.

CHAPTER IX.

A SURPRISE FOR MR. JELLIPOT

AS HE descended to the street, Inspector Combridge thought quickly. He knew nothing of the young man, whose business might be of the most innocent character, and whom, in any event, he might question to little purpose, knowing no more of him than he did now. Would it not be better to watch for him as he would leave the house, follow him without arousing his suspicions, and ascertain his identity before discovering his own knowledge of the call two days earlier which Mrs. Collis had thought too unimportant to mention—or had concealed for a reason of another kind? Anyway, the concealment was hers, and it was almost certainly expedient that she should be tackled first; and he would prefer to know a bit more than he did now when he put the question.

So he waited, concealed in the porch, watching for the young man, who had been asked in by Mrs. Collis, to reappear. When he did so, the inspector had realised that he might be about to waste time in finding out no more than a simple question would elicit at once, and which would prove to be of no importance to him. But he knew himself well enough to be aware that his reputation had been established by pertinacity of pursuit rather than any brilliance of deductive reasoning, and, though he doubted, his purpose held.

He had not waited long, for the young man came out again within a few minutes, and went off at a rapid pace, looking neither to right nor left. Anyone easier to follow (if quick walking were no obstacle) would not be simple to find.

He walked on briskly for five minutes, till he came to Portman's Restaurant, into which he turned. After a moment of hesitation, Inspector Combridge followed. He would be recognised by the head waiter. He would be recognised by either of the Reeves girls, if they should be there, as he was inclined to expect. But Portman's is free to all who can pay its bills. His curiosity was roused, and he was determined to know more. He went in.

It was too late for lunch. It was far too early for dinner. Portman's, which does not specialise in the serving of teas, was almost empty. He saw nothing of Blake, who was off duty. He saw nothing of Muriel or Arabella, who were not there.

He ordered a coffee he did not want, and observed that his quarry, still appearing unconscious of pursuit, after a moment of impatient hesitation, did the same.

As he drank, he studied the young man, whose eyes were restlessly on the door, but passed over him as though he were not there. Anyone less like a murderous criminal, or an associate of malefactors, it would be hard to imagine; but the inspector reminded himself that there are no criminal types.

More disconcertingly, he was becoming sure—or almost sure—that he had seen the young man somewhere before, though no mental effort would recollect where it had been.

He was going now. It had been no more than a ten minutes' stay. There was some more quick walking to be done next.

But it was not for long. This time, the young man mounted a city bus, and an opportune red light enabled the inspector to join him a moment later.

When they alighted at the stop which is only a few yards from Basinghall Street at its southern end, a surprising, rather uneasy doubt came to the inspector's mind, which changed to certainty a moment later, when the young man, approaching number 72A as one who had been there before, ascended by the lift to Mr. Jellipot's first floor offices.

Inspector Combridge, still disregarded, was so close behind that the lift man delayed for him to enter. But he hung back. He wanted a moment to think it out.

The result of this cogitation was that he decided: "I'll wait till he leaves. I'll find out who he is, and what it means before I make a fool of myself questioning him. There's a simple explanation, of course. And yet why did both Jellipot and Mrs. Collis conceal from me that he had been to Antrobus Road that morning? And Jellipot's got a theory I wouldn't believe! No wonder, if he's got knowledge like this that he doesn't share. But I've got more than a theory now. If this young fellow's as innocent as he looks, it's handcuffs for Robert Ames—and there'll be a better reason for not holding the coroner's inquest tomorrow than I expected to be able to show."

But the young man did not come down, and so at last Inspector Combridge went up to Mr. Jellipot's suite, and was confirmed in the wisdom of discretion when he saw the object of his pursuit seated at a desk in the outer office, and recognised him at last as one whom he had casually seen in that room before. This might explain much, but not all.

And so, being still puzzled, and having a very considerable respect for his opponent (if such Mr. Jellipot could be considered), when he found himself next moment in that gentleman's presence, he was still cautious in his approach.

He said: "There's an old lady living opposite Number Forty-Eight, who was watching the door (or so she says) all the morning that the murder occurred. She claims to have seen everyone who went in or out during that time."

"If you think her reliable, you may consider that you have obtained evidence of great—perhaps of decisive—importance, even though it be of no more than a negative character."

"It wasn't exactly negative."

Mr. Jellipot looked surprised. "I will confess," he said, "that on any theory of the crime which I had been able to form, I should have anticipated that its value could only have been of that description."

"Which is saying that you think Ames did the job? Well, I wouldn't say you're far wrong on that. I only meant there were other callers whom Mrs. Collis didn't mention, which ought to be made a headache for her. And there was one among them I needn't name because you know it already."

Mr. Jellipot looked puzzled. "I can assure you," he said, "even at the risk of appearing duller than I am normally, that I have no such knowledge, nor can I make any guess of what you may mean."

"Well, I mean the young man who's been there again this morning."

"I sent Tudor there this morning, with a message for Miss Reeves. If you are alluding to that—"

"If he's the young man outside now—"

"Tudor is a clerk who has been articled to me for the past two years. As to his being outside now, it is open to doubt. But I have none that he was there when you came in."

"Well, he was in the house almost as soon as Ames left. I don't suppose I'm telling you anything you don't know, and I'm not saying he had anything to do with the crime, but I do think I should have been told."

"Obviously so—if it be true. But will you accept my word that, if it were, it was entirely outside my knowledge? Beyond that, I regard it as most improbable. I think it more likely that your old lady witness is suffering from some confusion of mind."

"I don't think it was that. But it's easy to ask him."

"That, unless he have already left, is what I am proposing to do."

Mr. Jellipot picked up the telephone, and said that he would like Mr. Tudor to come in for a moment. Having listened to the reply, he laid it down with the explanation: "I am sorry, but he has just left. I should add that, before you came in he had asked to leave early this afternoon on some private business, and I had given that permission. Perhaps you will now tell me in more detail what you have learned."

Mr. Jellipot listened to the narrative which followed with his usual patient attention. At its conclusion, he said: "And, in view of this lady's evidence, you feel that you would be justified in arresting Ames? Well, I don't say you are wrong. To regard the crime as being the possible act of either Tudor or the butcher would be absurd. That any butcher should cut a customer's throat in an absent-minded moment, from mere force of habit, is, in itself, a proposition which may be held to fail in reasonable probability; and in this particular case there is an absence of any reason why he should have gone up to the bedroom at all. Had it been the housekeeper's throat—but it is a theory which we may put aside. Even that Mrs. Collis should have employed him for such a purpose is of an almost fantastic improbability. And, for quite different, but no less formidable reasons, you may eliminate Reginald Tudor also. My only doubt is as to whether you can be right that Reginald was in Antrobus Road that morning at all, and, in consequence, to what extent you can rely upon the accuracy of Mrs. Fishwick's memory. But if you are satisfied on that point—"

"Oh, he was there all right."

"Still, you may prefer to have his own account of the matter, and to clear up some other loose ends, however irrelevant they may prove to be, before taking decisive action."

"No. I don't know that I shall. We find things come out a lot faster after we've got the man we want under lock and key. And when we're as sure as I am here—"

"Yes. I know your theory. It is a matter on which you have more experience than I can claim, and I do not say you are wrong. Do you intend to make the arrest at once?"

"I'd like to know what time he usually leaves the works."

"I suppose he would be there now. It may be more doubtful whether you could get there before he would have left."

"Would you mind having him rung up, and asked to wait for me there?"

"You think that is wise?"

"You mean he might try a bolt? I shouldn't mind that. It would be just luck for us. He wouldn't get far."

"And he would have demonstrated his guilt to the satisfaction of any probable jury? Again, you may be right. Newman shall telephone him now, and let you know the result."

Five minutes later, Inspector Combridge was on the way to the Kilburn business premises of Messrs. Briggs & Co., electrical engineers and contractors, as rapidly as a taxi could make its way through the London traffic. He had not actually decided upon the arrest of Robert Ames, but he was resolved to invite him to accompany him to police headquarters, which is a distinction the difference of which is not always considerable.

CHAPTER X.

AN INVITATION DECLINED

ROBERT AMES sat in the office of the business over which he presided with little supervision, though, until two days before, it had had two proprietors, of whom he was not one.

Twenty minutes earlier, he had learned that Inspector Combridge would be on the way to interview him. Whether he were innocent or guilty of an employer's death, he could not be unaware that suspicion had gathered darkly about his head. He could see it in the eyes of those around him. He could hear it in the things they said, and still more was it silently evident in those which they did not say.

Even Miss Marchant, whom he had taken twice to the pictures in recent weeks, and who may have seen in these occasions a prelude to more significant familiarities—even her bold eyes would not meet his own, and her smile was gone.

Yet he had shown no sign of perturbation at this surrounding atmosphere. He had gone on managing the business with his usual bustling efficiency. He had sustained a previous interrogation from Inspector Combridge without being shaken in any material particular in the statement of his morning interview, as he had first given it, before (if he were innocent) he could have had any knowledge of the tragedy which had occurred. He had said, with a disarming frankness, that he could see that he must be under some measure of suspicion until the murderer should be found; and that he was anxious, for that and other reasons, that the police should prove equal to the discovery of the guilty man. But he owned that he could make no helpful suggestion. It was a baffling affair to him.

Now he had been using the half-hour interval before the inspector could arrive to clear up the details of the day's business, with his usual rather fussy energy. He signed his letters, with particularity in reading them over, and insistence upon a statement of no great importance being verified from the books before he would pass it.

Anything less like the attitude of one who intended to take to perilous flight could not be easily imagined. Had Inspector Combridge been invisibly present, the fear—or rather hope—that he might attempt to avoid arrest by that means would have left his mind.

Having dealt with these matters, he sat a few moments in silent thought. He turned out his pockets, burnt one or two papers, with no care that they should be entirely consumed, examined the contents of his wallet, and having counted the eleven one-pound notes it held, put ten of them into a drawer of the safe which he kept for personal use.

If he had any thought of arrest—which could hardly appear less than possible, even to an innocent man—he did no more than was prudent, in facing a legal system which, while it professes to regard all men as innocent till their guilt be proved, does not therefore protect property which may be on their persons from the prying hands, and temporary detention, of the police.

Having done this, and wandered restlessly round the office, as though fearful that there might be something he had overlooked, he sat, in a quietude unusual to him, for the few further minutes which remained before Inspector Combridge arrived.

"Well," he said, offering a hand which the inspector did not refuse, though his response was feeble, "take a seat. I hope you've come to tell me that you've found out what we're all anxious to know."

"I have obtained some further evidence. But I'm sorry to say that it appears to reduce the possibility that anyone who could have committed such a crime called at the house between when you left and when Mrs. Collis entered the room."

Mr. Ames appeared not to observe the implication of this. He said: "I suppose you often have these setbacks, before you get at the truth."

"Well, we usually do get to the truth at last."

Inspector Combridge looked at a man he had disliked from the first moment he saw him, and was disturbed by a momentary doubt of whether he were allowing himself to be biased by that dislike. It was a natural antipathy between two men whose similarities and differences were alike of antagonising kinds.

The inspector's hair was red, and so was that of Ames, though of a more emphatic shade. But the inspector's was close-cropped, and neatly kept. That of Ames looked as though its last combing might be two days, and its last cutting two months before.

Ames' waistcoat was half unbuttoned. There was no crime in that. But neither was there any suggestion of incongruity. He had the appearance of a man whose waistcoat at any time would be unbuttoned more likely than not.

"We shall have to ask you," the inspector said, "to sign a statement setting out the facts as you have already given them to us verbally. It is for that purpose that I am obliged to ask you to come with me now. But I ought to warn you that anything you say further, or which you may consent to sign, may be used in evidence."

Mr. Ames' eyebrows rose. "That's putting it straight, isn't it? If it's not saying I killed Briggs, it's going about halfway. But you know, apart from anything else, I hadn't any motive. Not the least. And men don't commit murders without any quarrel, and no motive at all.

"So, however awkward it looks for me, I can tell you that I'm not really afraid. But, of course, I'll sign the statement. I've told you what happened, and I've no more to say, bad or good. If you'll just wait while I get my coat and a wash—shan't be five minutes—I'll come with you now."

"Well," the inspector replied, "be as quick as you can. I've got a taxi waiting for us outside."

Ames made no reply. He went out of the room, leaving the door carelessly open behind him. Combridge saw him enter a door marked Private, on the opposite side of the passage. As it opened, there could be seen the white gleam of a hand basin against the wall. The Inspector sat patiently for five minutes. He sat impatiently for three more.

Then he got up. Was the fool committing suicide? He was conscious that his own course of conduct had been such as the occasion required; but, all the same, if such a thing *had* occurred, it would not be considered a credit to him. He went to the door of the lavatory. He tried the handle, and found it to be bolted or locked. He called: "Mr. Ames, shall you be long?"

There was no reply. He called louder, and then changed his tone. "If you don't answer, I shall break the door."

There was still silence. From a door farther down the passage, two girls came out. They had hats and coats on, evidently prepared to leave. They watched half curious, half afraid.

Inspector Combridge called to them: "Tell someone to bring an axe."

They stood irresolute, and he decided to try what he could do. The door did not look very strong.

He put his weight against it, and felt it give; kicked with his full strength, and a puny bolt gave way, so that the door flew wide open. He looked into a small empty room.

Where could Ames have gone? Not through the window. A boy of ten might have stuck fast in that narrow space. But there was a closed door on the right hand, locked, and with no handle on that side. It appeared to be disused, but was the obvious explanation of the empty room.

It was harder to open, giving way at last to a key from another door, one of those which the young women, whose curiosity had overcome their preliminary hesitation, had collected at his request. But the inspector's mind was now comparatively at ease. He was not surprised to find that the door led to a women's lavatory, which opened on to another passage, with a warehouse on its further side.

He said to the two girls, who were now following in a state of giggling excitement: "You can get off home now. There'll be nothing more doing here tonight."

"We can't go without locking the front door."

"Then you'll have to wait while I phone."

With the ready help of one of the girls, he was soon through to Superintendent Roomer, who heard his narrative with a chuckle of satisfaction. "It's a bit of trouble for us now," he said, "but it'll save a lot more in the end."

He rang off to issue the instructions which within half an hour would rouse the whole force of the Metropolitan Police to an alert watch for the missing man, and, a little later, those within a far wider area. He had no doubt that he would see Ames brought in within twenty-four hours, if not twelve. He felt that, short of a written confession, the man had given the police all the assistance he could.

CHAPTER XI.

REGINALD SAYS LITTLE

"I HEAR," Mr. Jellipot said, with his usual mildness, "that you called at Mr. Briggs' house on the morning of the murder, and were there for some time."

Tudor flushed slightly, but looked at his employer without flinching as he replied: "If I were, sir, it wasn't on the firm's business."

"And it is therefore not mine, you would like to say? But if it were not on the firm's business, should it have been done in the firm's time?"

"I was working very late on the previous night."

"Or you might have gone then? It is a substantial excuse, though the formality of obtaining my consent need not have been omitted. I might have been content with what you have said, but Inspector Combridge will want to know more."

"Then Inspector Combridge can go to hell."

Mr. Jellipot looked slightly surprised at the emphatic nature of this reply, and even more so did the young man from whose mouth it came.

"I beg your pardon, sir," he said. "I didn't mean to speak like that, but it's no business of his."

"It was an irrelevant observation, the final destination of Inspector Combridge not being the subject with which we dealt. You must appreciate that you entered the house, if I be informed correctly, almost immediately after Mr. Ames left, and that a serious crime had just occurred, or would occur there in the next hour. Such a position is certain to arouse the curiosity of the police."

"If I know nothing about it, I can't help them; and if I went there to cut his throat, I'm not likely to say."

"It is less simple than that, there being many intermediate possibilities. You are certainly not obliged to make any statement in-

49

criminating yourself. But I do not suppose that that question can seriously arise."

"It would be cockeyed nonsense to think I went there to kill Briggs."

"Perhaps so. But suspicion is regarded as duty in the efficient ranks of the C.I.D. I have reason to think that I have not been entirely free from it myself, either in the mind of Inspector Combridge or Mr. Quigley."

Tudor laughed. "Well, of course, if they think I did it during office hours, they might suppose it was on instructions from you. But it would be in the diary, if so. I should think there'd be a fat fee to charge up against the client whose instructions we were carrying out."

"It has a humorous side which you are not slow to observe. But it would not have been on the instructions of others, but for my own benefit that I should have been acting. There was an unfortunate possibility that I might have benefited under a will which, I am glad to say, was not made."

"You think...?" The young man checked himself abruptly. "No," he concluded, "I'd say you needn't worry about that!"

"I am not. It might exceed fact to say that I have been worried at all. But I am inclined to think that you know more of this matter than you have yet said."

There was a moment of silence, and then Mr. Jellipot went on with unaltered placidity: "Which you admit when you do not deny. But I will not press you for a confidence which you are reluctant to give. If you have reason to suppose that Mr. Briggs died intestate, I may, however, mention that it is no more than I have known since yesterday morning."

But Reginald still made no reply. His eyes, which had been lifted frankly, were now fixed on the ground.

"Well," Mr. Jellipot concluded, "we must leave it there. But you will treat the inspector with greater confidence, if you will take the advice of an older man. Think it over while you have time."

"Yes, sir, I certainly will."

With this assurance, and some return to his earlier manner, Reginald left the room; and, almost immediately after, Inspector Combridge was announced.

CHAPTER XII.

INSPECTOR COMBRIDGE HAS NO REPLY

"You haven't caught him yet," Mr. Jellipot commented, as the inspector concluded his narrative of the events of the previous evening, "but you feel confident that you will?"

"It's about a thousand to one. I don't say I'd take it on even at those odds unless I'd got a quid that I shouldn't miss. We'll have his picture in the afternoon papers, and there'll be a few million people besides the police who'll have their eyes on any stranger who comes their way.

"It isn't ever easy hiding from the police, even if a man's got plenty to spend. Ames may have that—I don't know. But he hasn't drawn anything much lately from his own bank. We've found that out already. But even if he has, it doesn't make much difference. Not in a case like this.

"You see, it isn't as though we're after one of the criminal class. They've got friends of their own kind. They know where to go. But he won't. He'll be like a fox with no hole. If he gets a week's run, he'll be a lot luckier than they often are."

"Don't they ever have a hiding place ready beforehand?"

"I never met such a case. And if you think it out, it isn't a likely thing. They don't murder anyone with a plan of bolting and losing everything. They think they're going to manage a lot better than that. It's afterwards that they get frightened and lose their nerve."

"I have no doubt you are right. Though how Ames could have done it, and thought that suspicion would pass him by, is not easy to understand. But you did not come—or did you?—only to tell me this."

"No. I came to have a few words with young Tudor."

"Which it was very natural to wish to do. But does the occasion remain? You consider—I am not suggesting that you are wrong—that Ames has practically pleaded guilty by flight. If—or should I say when?—you catch him, you may obtain a more formal confession. When you have it, will you not be better able to judge whether anything that may have happened later in the morning can be of importance to you to know?"

Inspector Combridge did not answer at once, but he looked stubborn, and Mr. Jellipot went on in his more persuasive manner: "You have some reason to think that both Mrs. Collis and the Misses Reeves have lied to you, whether from the same or quite different reasons is hard to guess. Naturally, you resent this. But if you pursue inquiries which have ceased to be material to your case, and you are further rebuffed, will you not be asking for what you get? In any event, you have no complaint against Tudor, whom you have not interrogated."

"And you think I'd better leave it at that? Well, you may be right; and, anyway, it will keep. But all the same...." He got up, leaving the sentence uncompleted. He had an uneasy feeling that Jellipot had more motive than he disclosed. And yet, was it not sense?

If Ames should offer any explanation or defence which involved the subsequent movements of those people—and yet how could he?—there would be time to pursue such enquiries. Until then....

Changing the subject, he said: "We hear that Gilson's at the Briggs works this morning, taking charge as though he'd been there all his life. He hasn't lost any time."

"With his interest in the business, and being the only one left, it sounds to me to be a very natural and necessary thing to do."

"Oh, of course. I'm not saying anything against him."

"Actually, he has already telephoned that he will be coming to see me. He says there are matters connected with the business on which he will require legal advice."

"Well, he'll be coming to the right place."

"So we must hope," Mr. Jellipot replied, in the tone of one whose mind is on other things. He added: "It is one of the most puzzling cases I ever met."

The inspector looked surprised. "That's how I felt about it till yesterday. But it's straight ahead for us now, with the signal down."

"Yes. It is a natural point of view. But what motive can Ames have had?"

The inspector had no answer to that. Indeed, its effect was that he went away with a vague disquiet which his reason told him that he had no occasion to feel. But this feeling would have found little relief had he been supernaturally endowed with power to overhear a conversation which was then proceeding, in the confidence of the packing room which they shared, between the two girls who had given him their assistance on the previous evening.

"Don't you think we ought to tell the police?"

"No, I don't. I think it would be just horrid. I don't want him to get hanged. Anyway, not through me. And, besides, how could we without...?"

Yes. How could they without...? The other girl saw that. And after all, the police should be able to manage their own affairs. They went on packing micrometers with the deft fingers that practice gives.

CHAPTER XIII.

MORE CALLERS FOR MR. JELLIPOT

MR. GILSON said: "He was a man I never liked. But I can't see now what motive he could have had."

Mr. Jellipot agreed: "But it is a matter which may be cleared up when he has to defend himself."

Mr. Gilson hardly saw that. Was it likely that a man would offer a motive for doing that which he would be sure to deny?

Mr. Jellipot agreed again, but said that it is often through the dissection of lies that the truth will become clear.

Mr. Gilson did not pursue the subject. He had more urgent matters upon his mind. Having disposed of others of more immediate importance, he asked whether Mr. Jellipot had heard anything of the dispositions of the dead man's will.

"I have reason to believe," Mr. Jellipot replied, "that no will was made."

Mr. Gilson looked sceptical. "Ames," he said, "told me differently. I think you will find that a will was executed about a fortnight ago."

"Then I am afraid that he was not accurately informed. My information (which is derived from the solicitors who were acting for Mr. Briggs in that matter) is that there was a delay for obtaining of counsel's opinion upon some of its contemplated provisions, and that it was unsigned in consequence. If Ames committed the murder under the presumption that those provisions would be beneficial to himself (which, however inadequate it may seem, is the only motive that can be surmised), it was a most pointless crime."

Mr. Gilson took this information without appearing to be greatly perturbed, though he expressed a natural disappointment.

"I had understood," he said, "that the whole of the insurance money would have been available for the development of the business, which I should naturally have welcomed, but I suppose that it will still benefit to a substantial extent."

"That appears to be so. I have already referred to the terms of the partnership deed, and to the balance sheet which was attached thereto.

"The business will, in the first instance, receive the benefit of the insurance money, that being the intention with which you stipulated that the policy should be taken out.

"But your obligation to acquire your partner's interest, if you decide to continue trading, will naturally remain, and the addition of the insurance money to the business assets places it in a position of substantial solvency, in which Briggs' estate must share.

"I estimate that this interest will amount to about £11,500. To that extent the business will lose by the fact that the will was not executed, but it will still benefit by the introduction of over £8,000, and the proprietorship will be entirely yours.

"It is evident that your prudence in stipulating for the taking out of the policy has been justified by the course of events."

"Yes. I should have been in the devil of a mess. I might have had to close."

"You are intending to carry on?"

"Yes. My own business isn't one that ties me down. It's almost all correspondence. I've been used to doing most of it in the evening, and seldom been at the office more than two or three hours a day. And Briggs and Co. will be a good business with that capital behind it. You know I've always had that opinion. I don't say that Briggs won't be missed. He was a genius in his way. But there are as many patents now as anyone could wish to have, and you know he did next to nothing at the works. He sometimes didn't enter the doors for weeks, and Ames did more or less as he liked. There'll be a bit more order and method there now."

"Yes. I expect there will."

Mr. Gilson spoke in the tone of one who opens a window to let in sunshine and better air, and as Mr. Jellipot listened he was conscious of liking him a little more than he had done previously, which had not been much.

He noticed that he spoke of Ames in the past tense. Well, that was natural enough. Even if he should not be convicted of murder, his abrupt departure might excuse the man who would soon be the sole proprietor from continuing to employ him. And Gilson, though he had exonerated Ames from suggestions of financial malpractice, had never liked him. He had made no secret of that.

As Mr. Gilson went out, Mr. Jellipot glanced at the clock. It was already past midday, and so far his time had been entirely occupied with the affairs of the murdered man, to the exclusion of other matters which should not be neglected longer. It was with an exclamation of impatience unusual to him that he heard next moment that Miss Reeves was waiting.

"Show her in," he said, after a second of hesitation, "but if anyone else should call, you will say that I am engaged until after lunch."

Having fortified himself thus against later intrusions, he received Muriel with his usual quiet cordiality. Separated from her sister's more vivid personality, it might not have occurred to anyone to regard her as deficient either in vitality or attractive features.

She had a long envelope in her hand, which she laid on the solicitor's desk as she said: "We thought I'd better bring Uncle's will to you."

"I am afraid," he replied, "that it will be of no legal value, though it may indicate what your uncle's wishes were, and there is always the possibility that those who become entitled to the estate may wish to fulfil them. But I have already heard that it was not legally executed when he died."

"It isn't quite like that. Uncle said if they couldn't do what they were told without all that fuss, he'd see what he could do himself."

As she offered this explanation, Mr. Jellipot had drawn a foolscap sheet from the envelope. He turned it over, and, to his experienced eyes, it had the look of a good will. The signature was certainly that of Robert Briggs. There were the names of two witnesses—Muriel Reeves and Reginald Tudor—under the usual formula of joint presence. He raised momentary eyebrows at the second name.

"Is this," he asked, "Mr. Tudor's doing?"

"No. Nothing at all. Except I asked him to oblige Uncle by signing."

"Do you benefit in any way under the will?"

"No. We didn't want to, Belle or I. We've got plenty."

"I only asked because, had it been otherwise, you would have lost that benefit by being a witness, which sometimes happens when wills are drawn up without legal advice. Well, I will deal with this." He laid the will aside, and continued: "There was the other matter on which I sent a message to you by Mr. Tudor yesterday. It may have become of less importance since the police have decided that Ames is responsible for the crime, and that enquiries in other directions are no longer necessary. But you may like to tell me what the situation was which it may still become necessary to explain."

"It was kind of you to send the message you did, but I don't think there is anything we really need say about it."

"Possibly not. But there is reliable evidence that your sister was in London at a time when she was supposed to be in Cornwall. There is a reasonable presumption that she did not go to Cornwall at all. We may conclude that she was in London at the time of the murder, and that there has been something approaching a conspiracy to conceal that fact from the knowledge of the police."

"I suppose lots of people would think that."

"Which is a polite way of telling me that my interference is not desired?" Mr. Jellipot queried, with no reduction in the friendliness of his tone. "May I conclude that that attitude is one in which your sister concurs?"

"Belle said, if anyone tried to get anything out of me, I was to answer in two words. But I couldn't say 'So what?' to you. It would sound ruder from me than it would from her."

Mr. Jellipot recognised the truth of that. Spoken with Arabella's bright eyes and smiling lips, and in a voice which it was music to hear, the words might be innocent of offence, but their meaning would still be there.

"Well," he said, "I daresay you can both take care of yourselves. I must see what can be done with this." He shook hands as he took up the will.

CHAPTER XIV.

MR. JELLIPOT READS THE WILL

MR. JELLIPOT had no difficulty in deciding that the will was good. It contained one or two phrases at which he winced, but even in its wording there was little to which criticism could be directed, for most of it was copied from Mr. Coote's draft, and Mr. Jellipot respected that gentleman's legal abilities.

Its provisions were simple in their intention, though difficult to define to the satisfaction of the professional mind. The unusual idea, in the absence of greedy natural heirs, of benefiting a solicitor to whom the testator felt he had cause to be grateful, appeared to have been overcome by the discouragement which it had received. The intention of the present will was that the whole amount which might be realised from the estate should be devoted to the business, not as an investment, but as a donation to be explicitly expended upon the development of the Briggs inventions which it had been founded to produce and market.

Crudely considered, it was a gift to Gilson of over £11,000, in view of the certain value of the inventions with which it dealt. But it was evident that the exact limits of such expenditure would be hard to control, or even define. Mr. Jellipot approved the caution that had declined to accept responsibility without taking counsel's opinion, the exact effect of which is that neither of the legal gentlemen concerned had any responsibility at all.

Mr. Jellipot next observed, without gratitude, that he had been appointed an executor, to act jointly with Muriel and Arabella Reeves, with power to operate the proposed fund. In return for this, he was to receive a legacy of £200. The young ladies received no corresponding benefit. Natural affection for their deceased uncle was, he concluded, to be their sufficient incentive. (But what help, he thought, am I likely to get from them?)

He saw that Briggs, in his posthumous directions, as in his life, showed more interest in the production and perfecting of his creations than in the profits which they might earn. He had been commonly condemned for conduct arising from that attitude. He had been called incurably lazy. (He had certainly been a late riser.) He had been called (with justification) a bad businessman. Ames had mentioned that he had once excused himself for not having appeared at the works on a day when he had definitely promised to be there, because it had been too fine a morning. Such were not the actions of prudent, provident men.

Yet Mr. Jellipot saw something here that he could admire. In the cant phrase, Briggs had had the defects of his qualities—and those qualities were not base. The thought deepened indignation at the brutal, unprovoked murder, and shut out any thought of sympathy for the hunted criminal.

There remained the question of who—of how many of those concerned—had known of the existence of this will? It had already become clear that both Ames and Gilson had supposed a will to exist. Gilson had been frank upon that. But supposition is less than certainty. Had Ames *known*? Had Gilson? Had both? If Gilson had, he had shown himself a good actor at the morning's interview. But more probably he had not.

Mr. Jellipot went out to a late and hurried lunch, feeling that he had given more than enough time to the Briggs affair, and that he must put it aside for the remaining hours of the business day, but when he returned Miss Arabella Reeves was already waiting to see him.

CHAPTER XV.

ARABELLA EXPLAINS

"I MEANT," Arabella said, "to come with Muriel, but she started without me. I thought I'd better see you about the will."

"I am always pleased to see you," Mr. Jellipot replied truthfully, for she was a girl he liked. "But there was no immediate hurry."

"I expect you've found time to read it?"

"Yes. I know what it contains."

"Is it a good will?"

"Yes. It will almost certainly be legally valid, if you mean that."

"So I was afraid."

"You mean you would like it to be bad?"

"Yes. I wish it were."

"Yet you witnessed it, and consented to be an executrix?"

"I thought I'd like to help you to make things as difficult as I can."

"To make things difficult? Forgive me, Miss Arabella, if I don't look upon it as a very attractive programme."

"Well, it's the best we can do."

"If you would make your intentions clear—"

"Well, I don't suppose you like Mr. Gilson, do you?"

"I have scarcely considered it necessary to define my feelings. He is a client; and certainly, if I should be acting in any matter in which he would be directly or indirectly concerned, I should not allow such feelings to influence me in either direction."

"Yes. I was afraid of that."

"Feeling so strongly as you appear to do, why did you not oppose your uncle in the making of this will?"

"Because he might have thought we wanted something ourselves."

"I see. And you thought he might make a mess of it, drawing it up himself, and that was the best chance that Ames or Gilson wouldn't get control of the money?"

"I hoped Mr. Gilson wouldn't."

"Why don't you like Mr. Gilson?"

"Well, I just don't. I suppose, if he were the one who killed Uncle, he couldn't benefit from the will?"

"You think he may have done it?"

"I don't know. I told the policeman I wasn't there. I said, 'if he did'."

"You are right in thinking that the law will not allow a man to benefit from his own criminal act. But the money being left in the way it is, I should not be prepared to advise that, even if Mr. Gilson should be convicted of the crime, it would vitiate the provisions of the will, whatever indirect benefit it might be to him as the proprietor of the business. Yet, under such a supposition—which I suggest that you should be careful not to discuss outside this room—he would doubtless be occupied in other ways."

"Yes. I see that." The girl's voice was as soft and pleasant as ever, but her satisfaction in the thought of how Mr. Gilson might be occupied was not concealed.

"There is just one thing," Mr. Jellipot said, "which I should like to ask while we are together now. You say that you were not there when your uncle was murdered. I have no doubt that that is so. But it is equally true, is it not, that you were not in Cornwall?"

"I was at the Regent Street Hotel."

"Should you think me rude if I ask why?"

"I don't mind telling you. Muriel knows now. Reggie had been chumming up to her, to get in with me. I stayed here to see him, and tell him where he got off."

"Which no doubt you did?"

"He knows a thing or two now."

"I've no doubt he does. And now, if you would explain to me with equal frankness why you suggest that Mr. Gilson is responsible for your uncle's murder, I shall be particularly interested, because, to be frank with you, I had understood from Inspector Combridge that you were disposed to condemn Mr. Ames in the same way."

"Well, I don't see why not."

"You mean that they may both have been partners to the crime, though one alone may have been the actual murderer?"

"And that seems silly to you?"

"I have not said so. It is a matter on which I have a very puzzled, but particularly open mind."

"Well, that's how I feel."

Mr. Jellipot made no direct comment upon this feminine attitude. He said: "I understood some months ago that you did not trust Ames, and had tried to arouse your uncle's suspicions. Now you regard Mr. Gilson with an equal distrust. Can you say that you have any valid reason for that?"

"The beast wants to marry Muriel."

It was an unexpected reply, and Mr. Jellipot did not conceal his surprise. He asked: "Is there any reason for anticipating such an event?"

"There wasn't while she thought Reggie was after her. I'm not so sure now."

"I see how you feel. We must hope that the question will not arise in an acute form, and particularly not before responsibility for the murder has been resolved. I will do what I can."

With this promise, which was much for Mr. Jellipot to give, and was to cause him some sleepless hours in the night, he shook hands, and Arabella left with a feeling of relief for which we may fail to see any evident cause.

CHAPTER XVI.

MR. JELLIPOT HAS A DIFFICULT INTERVIEW

MR. JELLIPOT'S hope that Inspector Combridge would be proved right in his anticipation of the prompt arrest of Robert Ames was not realised.

His continued liberty became a matter to which much newspaper space was devoted, and many theories were advanced among which that which became most generally held, and was most popular at Scotland Yard was that he must have committed suicide. This may be done in ways by which the discovery of the body may be precarious or delayed, without any reflection upon the vigilance of the police. The search had been so promptly begun, and had been so thorough, that it did not seem possible that it could have been evaded in any other way.

And this theory was supported by the fact that the man seemed to have made no preparations for flight, and to have taken no money with him. It was true that some investments, of no great amount, had been realised within the past year, and that the money they had brought in could not be clearly traced, but, beyond that, his bank account showed little but credits for his monthly salary cheque, and money drawn out each week to a yearly corresponding total. It appeared, and was readily confirmed by Gilson, that the £500 loan to the firm, which had been repaid, had been reinvested in the business at Ames' particular request. He had explained (Gilson said) that he no longer held the shares in connection with which he had thought that it would be required, and his confidence in the business, after it had received the support of Gilson's capital, had become such that there was no form of investment he would prefer.

Anyway, there it was.

A search of his Bayswater lodgings, which were as untidy as himself, did not suggest that he had taken such things away as a fleeing man would be likely to need. An exhaustive enquiry for rela-

63

tions, near or far, to whom he might have gone, disclosed only two aunts, of whom one was dead, and one was living in Chelsea on a small annuity which he appeared to have given her some assistance in purchasing ten years earlier. Her evidence was of a negative character. She had not seen him for years. She could not give the address of any other living relative. Inspector Combridge, reporting his interview with her to Superintendent Roomer, said unkindly: "She doesn't seem to know anything about him. I should say she knows a lot more about senile decay."

With patient thoroughness, he had examined the business staff, and gained nothing there beyond some light upon how Ames had spent his salary, which, in view of its amount, and his manner of living, had not been simple to see.

He had a hint from Miss Marchant, a young woman to whom the missing man had made such advances as had caused her to calculate, in a cool, avaricious mind, whether she could make a major profit by bidding for matrimony, or would be wiser to take what she could get on mutually easier terms; and who was not pleased to think that it was a throat-cutter to whom she had so nearly confided her very saleable self. She said that the packing room girls could tell him something, if anyone could.

The packing room girls, examined together and then separately, evidently had something to tell, though it might not be useful to the police to know. Their nervousness was apparent. But they said nothing which Inspector Combridge could see to be any use to him. If he had asked the right questions, he might have got some startling replies, but that was something he would be most unlikely to do. They were relieved when they were released from enquiries which had not been as bad as they had feared. Nothing like! And they could feel that they had given truthful replies, which some girls in their positions might have objected to do. Ames had gone, and the world went on much the same. Some snatch-and-grab raids in the West End drew the inspector's attention away.

Meanwhile, Mr. Jellipot had found himself faced by another aspect of the position which had been produced by that still legally uncertain hand which had used Adrian Briggs' razor to its owner's destruction. The financial position of the Southern and General Assurance Co. had not improved, and though a single claim, even for £20,000, might not seem sufficient to be of decisive importance, it was an added weight in a trembling scale.

Mr. Jellipot had to interview the Chairman of the London & Northern Bank on the Company's behalf, and, though he had the advantages of being solicitor to the bank, and a personal friend of Sir Reginald Crowe, he had a very difficult time.

"I tell you, Jellipot," Sir Reginald said irritably, "it's the sort of account that I won't have. I'll do more than most to help any business that's in a genuine difficulty that it couldn't have been expected to have foreseen. You know that well enough. And especially so if they're frank with me. But Quigley isn't. He's tricky. And he's underwritten risks that a sounder man would have left alone, and he's found it a gamble that didn't pay. I'll let the overdrafts stand as they are for three months, and there'll have to be regular reductions after that. That's my last word. And if they try to draw sixpence over that limit, the cheque will go back, and you know what that would be certain to mean for them."

"Then I should be disposed to advise immediate liquidation."

"You think it's as hopeless as that?"

"I don't think it's hopeless at all. But I think that such a rule, strictly applied, would be certain to lead to a position to which that word would apply."

"Then you think Quigley isn't fit for his job?"

"You must forgive me declining to express an adverse opinion upon the managing director of my own clients. Suppose I should give you my own guarantee for £500 or £1,000?"

"What difference would that amount make to them? We're dealing with big figures here."

"If they should not know of the existence of the guarantee, and you would inform me of the first time that they should exceed your limit?"

"You must feel strongly about it to offer that. And it might work, but not twice. I suppose it's the Briggs' claim that's on your mind. But I can tell you that I wouldn't let them down over that. It's other things."

"Then you are saying that I introduced a client to an insurance company which is unsound. In that case, I should feel bound in honour to pay the claim from my own resources."

"Which would about empty the till?"

"I should not be ruined."

"Well, you're not going to do it. But I'll tell you one thing: Quigley will have to go."

"I was hoping that you would say that."

"I see. But the suggestion wasn't to come from you? And we must nominate one of our own men for the board. And I'll have a talk with their accountants, and, if I'm not satisfied, we'll make a change there. But if I tell you I'll see them through, you'll have to put off paying the Briggs claim for six months, if not more. You're quite equal to fixing that."

Mr. Jellipot admitted that it was not beyond the bounds of possibility that he would be able to do so.

Sir Reginald, after remarking with probable truth that there was no other man in London for whom he would have done so much, turned the conversation to the position of the second debenture holders in Wigan Mills Ltd., with which we have no present concern.

CHAPTER XVII.

MR. GILSON'S DECISION

MR. GILSON attended at Mr. Jellipot's office at the solicitor's request.

Mr. Jellipot said: "I am speaking both as solicitor for the Southern & General, and as an executor of the will of Adrian Briggs. You are aware that the liability of the Assurance Co. depends upon the question of whether Mr. Briggs died by his own or another hand.

"I will say frankly that there is no doubt in my own mind that it was a case of murder. Indeed, the murderer appears to have been particular to leave no doubt on that point, so that—"

"That was just how it looked to me."

"Then we agree. But it does not alter the fact that the death occurred before the reservation of the suicide clause had terminated by lapse of time—indeed, within a few weeks of the policy being taken out—and that, with such an amount involved, any insurance company would examine the evidence in a very critical and sceptical spirit.

"Generally, under such circumstances, they will be guided by the verdict of a coroner's jury, or by the jury of a criminal court. You will appreciate that, in a prosecution for murder, the defence will be sure to raise the issue of suicide if it be any way possible to do so, and that the jury's verdict may be decisive to approve or dismiss it.

"But in this case no inquest has yet been held, nor is any trial in process or pending—at least, unless Robert Ames can be found. Under these circumstances...."

"If you're going to suggest a compromise, I'll say at once that I don't think you ought to take a penny less than the twenty thousand."

"No I have a proposal which may be better than that. I have here a letter signed without prejudice by Mr. Sherwood, the acting manager—Mr. Quigley having resigned a few days ago—undertaking that the claim will be passed for full payment within six months of this date in the absence of any intervening legal development, which would, of course, be held to include any action brought by the estate against them within that period. Should I agree, there will, of course, be a binding contract to give effect to the offer made."

Mr. Gilson looked thoughtful. "Six months," he said, "is a long while."

"It is six months. A defended action, or even one that would be taken up to the eve of the hearing, might cause a longer delay, and such an undertaking as is offered would relieve us from the measure of uncertainty which all legal processes must involve."

"You advise acceptance?"

"The responsibility of decision rests primarily upon myself, and the young ladies who have an equal authority, but it is a matter in which you are most directly interested, and I should be very unlikely to act against your explicit wish."

"Well, I'd rather leave it to you. But it's no use talking about suicide. It's just bosh."

"I am disposed to agree. The murderer—whoever he may have been—appears to have gone out of his way, as I remarked before, to relieve us of any substantial ground for uncertainty on that point."

"So it looks to me."

"It makes it a very interesting problem."

"I wouldn't say interesting's the word," Mr. Gilson replied, with more show of irritability than had been induced by the news that the payment of the insurance money could not be expected immediately. "But the way things have gone has left the business on my hands, with no help from anyone, and I'll tell you what I've decided to do. I'm going to sell the stamp business—I've just sent off the advertisement—and concentrate on Briggs & Co. And when you know that, you'll understand that I don't mind how soon that insurance money's ready for use. I've got plans for expansion which will cost more than a bit."

"You have certainly lost no time in facing the position in which you have been so unexpectedly placed."

"Well, I'm a businessman."

Mr. Jellipot did not dispute that. He said: "I suppose you have no doubt that, in searching for Ames, the police are after the right man?"

Mr. Gilson did not exactly hesitate, but he paused slightly before replying. "I didn't like Ames. I didn't like some of his ways.

I've just had to sack his secretary, Miss Marchant, because she hinted that I didn't know what a secretary's really for, and that's a kind of thing I can't stand. But I can't see why Ames should have done it.

"All the same, the way he cleared out is next-door-but-one to pleading guilty, if it isn't nearer than that. Homicidal mania's the best guess I can make."

Mr. Jellipot said thoughtfully that that was certainly an idea, and Mr. Gilson went without further words.

He went back to the works, and had not been many minutes in his office when he was informed that one of the warehouse girls wanted to see him.

"Tell her to come in," he said casually, and then, as she entered, and stood for a moment in awkward silence: "Well, Clara, what is it?"

"I want to leave on Saturday."

Mr. Gilson looked at her intently. "Any reason?" he asked.

Her eyes were lifted to his for a moment, and then fell. She was still looking down as she answered sulkily: "I'm frightened. I don't like ghosts."

"Ghosts?" he echoed. "It sounds silly to me. But you know your own business best. How about Bessie?"

"Oh, she thinks I'm silly too."

"Then you can leave when you wish."

She went out, leaving her employer in a thoughtful mood.

After a time, he picked up the telephone, and asked to be put through to the advertisement department of the *Bazaar* to which he had sent the advertisement offering his stamp business for sale a few hours earlier. He instructed them to hold over the advertisement until further notice.

"Whatever goes," he said, half aloud, "I've got to fight against that."

CHAPTER XVIII.

BELLE WANTS TO KNOW

THE weeks passed, and Robert Ames was still a much-wanted and missing man. Mrs. Fishwick, watching from her opposite window, had the entertainment of seeing a jostling crowd push into No. 48 to inspect, and perhaps to bid for, the furniture of the murdered man; and to observe its disposal during the following day.

The Misses Reeves, being disinclined to leave London, and unable to continue in the now-vacant house, migrated to the Regent Street Hotel, where they engaged a small private suite, and it was only after they had done this, and might have been unable to cancel their bargain without some considerable financial penalty, such as it would have been foolish to incur on so slight a ground, that Arabella learnt, to her annoyance, if not that of her sister, that Henry Gilson had engaged a room on the same floor.

There was no evidence that this was more than coincidence, and it was not in itself without reasonable explanation. He had found that the long hours which he was now occupying at the Kilburn works, to which had to be added the claims of the stamp business which he could not entirely neglect, had rendered it inconvenient to go out every evening to his Streatham flat. He had not given it up. He would still be there at weekends. But, for other nights, he preferred the conveniences of hotel life, and the Regent Street, being appropriately situated between the two premises, had been a natural selection for him to make.

Anyway, so it was; and it was a fact which increased Belle's determination that the mystery of her uncle's murder should not remain unsolved. She saw that, while Ames could not be found, there might be a natural tendency on the part of the police to regard it as a matter on which no further enquiry could be usefully made. Other matters engaged their time. It might not be to their credit that a murderer should escape, but, if in fact he had, the less said the better. That might be good enough for them. It was not so for her.

She disliked Gilson. She particularly disliked the fact that his eyes should have turned in her sister's direction. She did not therefore conclude that he was guilty of complicity in the murder of Adrian Briggs, of which there was no evidence to support her doubt. But it was a matter she did not intend to leave unsettled, if any exertion on her part could resolve it. And perhaps most sisters would have felt the same, even without the antipathy which she admitted. A doubt of such a nature, however slenderly founded, is not comfortable to have.

Actually, his advances to Muriel had been of a very preliminary and tentative kind, but they had been such as most women are quick to see, and to interpret in the right way. They might develop quickly, if Muriel should show a disposition to move in the same direction.

That was a point on which Belle was unsure what to expect, which was not strange, for Muriel was unsure of her own mind. She had been hurt, both in her affections and pride, when Reggie Tudor had used her as a means of approach to her younger sister, and it was a feminine consolation to see admiration in other eyes. Now she saw Gilson crossing the hotel lounge, and her thought was: "If only he had rather more hair!"

With this passionless reflection, she followed her sister, who was already moving toward the lift, and they went up to their own suite, where dinner was about to be served.

It was as soon as their door had closed, and they had no more sentient auditor than the dumb waiter, that Arabella began: "I don't mean to leave Uncle's murder till I've found out who did it."

"I thought," Muriel replied reasonably, "that everybody agrees now that it was Mr. Ames. He almost admitted that, when he ran away."

"I don't want to think. I want to be quite sure."

"I don't see how you can, if he's never found."

"Well, why shouldn't he be? He must be somewhere."

Muriel showed no disposition to dispute this, and Arabella added: "Besides, why should he have done it? He had no reason to hate Uncle, and nothing to gain that's at all easy to see."

"There may be something we don't know."

"I expect there is. Quite a lot. That's what I mean to find out."

"I don't see how you can do more than the police."

"There may be something they haven't tried. If they don't know why anything happened, how can they tell there was only one in it?"

"Who could there be, except Mr. Ames?"

"There might be Mr. Gilson, for one."

Arabella looked closely at her sister as she said this, but, though it was met with the protest: "Oh, Belle, I don't think you ought to say that!" which was often on Muriel's lips, there was an absence of the indignation which she had feared to arouse.

"No," she replied, "that's what Mr. Jellipot said. But he wouldn't say I was wrong, and that's why I'm going to get him to help me now."

"You think he will?"

"I'm going to have a good try."

She paused, with a hesitation which rarely delayed anything she had an inclination to say, and her eyes were on her sister with even more than her usual directness, as she added: "I thought of asking Reggie to see what he could do."

Muriel's tone was flat as she replied: "I shouldn't think he'd refuse. But what good could he possibly be?"

"Oh, you never know."

The telephone rang as Belle said this, and she rose and went over to it. "Speaking of—angels," she exclaimed, "Reggie's in the hall. He wants to know whether he can come up."

"Well, of course. We'd better ring for some dinner, if he's come straight from the office."

"Yes," Belle said. "Ask him to come up." She remained at the instrument long enough to ensure a hospitable reception for the ascending visitor, and was scarcely back at the table when he appeared.

Reggie, who had come in some doubt of the reception which he would meet from whichever of the sisters he should be destined to see, and on an excuse which could expect to gain no more than a momentary interview, found himself received like an expected and most welcome guest. Muriel's quiet friendliness was unchanged, and Arabella seemed to have forgotten the blunt and hurtful words with which she had so disconcertingly "told him where he got off" when they had met at that hotel on the day before her uncle's life was so shockingly ended.

"Reggie," she said, with her usual directness, "we've been talking things over, and we want you to help us to find out who killed Uncle."

They were words which Reggie Tudor certainly had not expected to hear, and a protest of incapacity would not have been improbable from a modest tongue. But he was not slow of wit, and he had one object to which he was prepared to subordinate all (to him) less important matters. He saw the consequences of such an alliance far more clearly than how he was to proceed with its surprising programme. He said: "Oh, rather! You know you can count on me."

He was rewarded with Arabella's friendliest smile, which the most indifferent of mankind might have been pleased to meet. She said: "Well, we've just rung for some dinner for you. We thought you wouldn't mind staying to talk it over."

Reggie having made it clear that he had no objection to that, the talk proceeded to the conclusion of the meal, and some time beyond, with the result (among others) that it was only after he had left the hotel that he recollected that he had not delivered the letter which he had intended to use to excuse his call.

It fell into the nearest pillar box, which had been its natural destination. The young ladies could last till morning without receiving the formal document to which Mr. Jellipot had invited their signatures in connection with the probate of their uncle's will.

CHAPTER XIX.

THREE QUESTIONS FROM MR. JELLIPOT

MR. JELLIPOT dealt with the morning's correspondence with his usual scrupulosity. He had finished the distribution of such communications as could be dealt with by an efficient staff, and was considering those which he had reserved for personal attention, when he was interrupted by the entrance of Reggie Tudor, who asked diffidently: "Could you spare me a few minutes, sir?"

"From which question," the solicitor replied acutely, "I may conclude that my letter of yesterday to the Misses Reeves did not go through the post?"

Reggie blushed slightly at the implication of this remark, but took some dubiously-founded pleasure in replying: "No, sir. It was posted yesterday evening."

"Which," Mr. Jellipot replied placidly, "illustrates the fallibility of deductive reasoning. Are you also prepared to tell me that the subject of our conversation will not be the murder of Adrian Briggs?"

"Miss Arabella thought you might be able to give us one or two hints on how to go ahead.

Mr. Jellipot appeared to find an unusual difficulty in deciding upon the nature of his reply. "Yes?" he queried at last. "Or did you?"

"It was her idea, sir, but I felt sure she was right."

The reply reduced Mr. Jellipot to a further silence. He remembered a promise, and his promises were not lightly made. He asked: "What is your own theory?"

"I don't know what to think," Reggie replied frankly. "Ames was there, and he seems to have pleaded guilty by running away. Besides, I was there myself a few minutes later, and I didn't see anything of Gilson, which goes some way to support what he says himself, that he didn't call. And Mrs. Collis sticks out that she didn't let anyone else in. All the same, I can't see why Ames should have done it, or how he thought he was going to get off if he did."

"That has been precisely my own difficulty."

"So Miss Arabella thinks we ought to find out what really happened."

"Where the police have failed? It is a bold thing to attempt."

"We don't think the police are doing anything. They only care to get someone convicted."

"What you suggest may be less than completely true, but some truth may be there. How do you propose to proceed?"

"That's where I thought you might be able to give me some good advice."

"Then I cannot do better than to suggest that you should emulate the methods of Chief Inspector Combridge, whose pertinacity in questioning everybody who has been within half a mile or half an hour of the time and place with which he may be concerned will often obtain results which deductive reasoning would never reach."

Reggie stood undecidedly. He said: "Thank you, sir." But his tone implied disappointment. He thought that if that were all the help he would be destined to get from Mr. Jellipot, it was not much.

"I thought—we thought—" he began doubtfully, "that you might have some theory—something to give us a start...."

His voice trailed off, but he stood his ground. The thought came opportunely that he might begin to emulate the methods of the inspector, which Mr. Jellipot so warmly approved, before leaving the room.

He watched his employer through two long minutes of motionless silence. He saw him take a half sheet of paper, and pick up a pen, which he still delayed to use.

Mr. Jellipot fought a reluctance which most men feel. He did not wish to be thought a fool. He *might* be right. But he was not sure. And if he should be wrong, he would be made ridiculous by having proposed a solution which any sane man would dismiss without serious thought. But no less, if he were in Reggie Tudor's position, he knew the direction in which his enquiries would proceed, and the questions which he would ask. He was too honest with himself not to admit that. And there was his promise to Arabella. Slowly, he began to write.

"Tudor," he said, as he passed the sheet to his clerk, "I may be utterly wrong. I probably am. And in that case any advice from me is more likely to hinder than help. But, if I were in your place, I should interview everyone who has been associated with Ames, at whatever angle, in his business or private life, and I should endeavour to obtain replies to the three questions which I have written here."

Reggie read, and bewilderment was evident in his eyes, which changed to a measure of comprehension, though astonishment was still there, as he said: "Thank you, sir. Thank you very much."

Mr. Jellipot said: "I shouldn't be in a hurry to say that. The occasion for gratitude may not arise."

Reggie went; and the solicitor turned his attention to other things. "After all," he reflected philosophically, "I don't see why anyone need think me a bigger fool than I really am." But whether or not he were an outsize in fools was a point about which he was still uncertain.

CHAPTER XX.

BESSIE WOULD LIKE MORE

IT was Friday afternoon. Mr. Gilson was paying the foremen, and the office and warehouse girls, with his own hands, as had been the custom of Mr. Ames before him. The girl who had replaced Miss Marchant dealt with those of the manual workers. When Bessie came in, she took her money, and then said, in a bold tone, but with flickering eyes: "I thought you might be giving me a raise about now."

It appeared that Mr. Gilson thought differently. He said that her wages were already on the high side. "But," he said, "it was what Mr. Ames had arranged, and I have no intention of altering that." He reminded her that the girl who had replaced the ghost-ridden Clara was being paid ten shillings less.

"Mr. Ames," Bessie explained, "liked how we got on."

Mr. Gilson was tempted to retort: "How you got on his knee?" but he had the discretion not to say it aloud. He had his own opinion of the two girls who had gone, and of this one who remained, and he disliked their ways and their kind. Still, Bessie was intelligent and industrious. She knew her job well.

He temporised: "I have no complaint of your work. You can ask me again in a month's time."

Bessie withdrew, not looking pleased. She was still frowning as she put on her coat to go. She said something under her breath which Mr. Gilson would not have liked to hear.

It was about this time that Reggie Tudor sat with Muriel and Belle in their own rooms at the Regent Street, enjoying a good tea, and narrating the inconclusive results of enquiries, the stubborn patience of which, if not their measure of success, might have gained the approval of Inspector Combridge himself.

"So," he said, "it sums up to this. I've got quite a lot of data on Mr. Jellipot's first point, though I've no means of guessing whether it includes anything that he'll think it any use to know.

"I've tried to chum up to half the men at the works in their own pubs, and I've got four of them to talk, and I've heard what they saw of Ames, and what they thought of him; and I can't see how there can be anything there that helps us at all, unless it's the hints I got that some of the girls could tell me a lot more.

"I did better when I got round his flat. I heard what his habits were, and how there would be nights when he wouldn't be home at all, and others when he brought girls there. And once one of them who came down the stairs at about one A.M., more or less drunk, slipped and fell, and said she'd hurt herself too much to stand. And he had to get a taxi and lift her into it. She was shouting, and they remembered that she said something that showed that she came from his business place, and that he called her Clara when he told her to shut her jaw.

"Well, I found out who she was, and that she'd left since Gilson took control, or more likely he'd sacked her—I shouldn't blame him for that—and I found out where she lived, and the evening before last I looked her up.

"I thought a pound note would be enough to start a girl like that talking, and so it did up to a point, but not far enough."

Belle interrupted: "You should have given her more than that."

And Muriel protested: "Oh, Belle, you shouldn't say that. It was Reggie's money, not ours."

"Anyway, that's what I did," Reggie went on, "and she seemed willing to talk till I asked the questions that Mr. Jellipot wrote, and then she dried up, but so that she left me almost sure that she knows something she won't tell. I suppose I didn't ask them in the right way."

"What reply exactly did she give you?" Belle asked.

"I was just coming to that. She said: 'You'd better ask Bessie that. It's no use asking me.'

"I've found out since that Bessie is a girl she used to know at the works—one of her own kind, I suppose—who's still employed there. She lives off the top end of the Edgware Road—18, Puller Street—and I thought I'd look her up tonight, and see what I can get her to say."

"I believe you're going to succeed, where even the police seem to have given it up," Belle said. Her voice was always pleasant to hear, but, there was something in her eyes also which Reggie was glad to see. If Muriel saw it also she gave no sign. It could mean no more than the resignation of that which she knew she could never win.

"I said I'd have a good try," Reggie answered, "but there's a long way to go yet. And if I'm near anything now, you must thank Mr. Jellipot rather than me." He added, in a more diffident tone: "I did wonder whether one of you would like to come with me. You might get more out of her than I should, and there'd be a witness to what she says."

The sisters looked at each other, and Belle was the first to speak. "I think that might be a good idea. We'd have dinner late, when you get back, and talk it over together."

But Muriel rejected the implication of this remark. "No. You'd better go. You'd do better than I."

"I don't see why I should."

"Oh, you would! You'd know what to say."

"Indeed, I shouldn't. I've no idea how we could begin, or what excuse we could make for calling at all."

"Reggie'll know how to manage that."

Reggie, while admitting the difficulty of the occasion, could not deny that the last fortnight had given him some experience in such approaches. He added that perhaps they might both like to come. But it was agreed that that would be too many. And in the end Muriel's quiet persistence prevailed, and Belle was the one to go.

CHAPTER XXI.

Miss Butcher Is Slow to Speak

"I'M not sure now that it's wise for me to come," Belle said, as they got off the bus in the Edgware road. "You'd probably do a lot better alone."

"It's more likely I shan't do any good one way or other. I believe the best way would be to leave this to you from the start, and just listen in."

Rather to his surprise, Belle did not instantly reject this proposal. She said: "I don't know. But we shan't do much good if we talk in turns. It's always a bad way of getting out of a hole, or getting anyone else in. Suppose you let me have a try, and if we find I'm messing it up, I sit back, and your inning begins?"

"That suits me."

"Then I think I'll go straight to the point. Show her some cash, and see what we can get by that."

"You'll be able to judge that better when you see what kind of girl she is."

"Well, I thought we knew."

Reggie had sufficient sense not to dispute that, though their present knowledge seemed less to him than it obviously did to her.

With no more words they came to the house they sought, the outer appearance of which did not suggest that money would be an argument of no account.

The door was opened by a large slatternly woman, who said shortly, in reply to Belle's query of whether Bessie were in, that Miss Butcher was out.

Belle said: "Perhaps she won't be long? May we come in and wait?" But the woman made no motion to give them entrance to the dingy hall.

She said dubiously: "She mayn't be that long. But I don't know what she'd say if I let anyone in her room when she's away. Could you call again in an hour's time? What name shall I say?"

"The name doesn't matter. We may call later." Belle answered, and in the same second the door closed.

"Shall we try again, or give it up for tonight?" Belle asked, disappointment in her tone.

"Oh, we'll try again, if it won't be too late for you."

"I don't mind the time. But she may not be back then."

"Then we'll try to get in, and wait there."

"You certainly know how to persist."

"Well, it's the only way. You get on bit by bit. We've learnt something now."

"I don't see that."

"We've learnt that her name's Butcher, and we know she's in lodgings. She won't have a family butting in, or holding her back."

"Yes. There's something in that. Where shall we go now?"

"We might sit in a cinema. There's not much choice in this district. But there'll be no need. The girl's coming now."

Belle turned her eyes in the direction of his, and saw a young woman of rather better aspect than the account she had received, or the house she had just visited, led her to expect.

Reggie also, though lacking Belle's acute feminine vision, was disposed to compare her favourably with the bibulous Clara. She was neater, and he was vaguely aware that she was better dressed.

Belle looked at her figure, and if her thought had been articulated it would have been: "She makes the best of a bad job. She spends a lot on herself in her vulgar way. She likes pleasure. She likes spending. She'll be easy to bribe."

All this was instantaneous, as the girl became conscious of them. She knew them both, for they had been to the works on different occasions, and she had observed them, though they had taken no notice of her.

She made a quick movement to retreat, which she controlled as she realised that she was already seen. She came forward with what she meant to be an air of unconsciousness as she passed them, but Belle stood in her way.

"Miss Butcher," she said, in a voice that was like a gentle caress, in which there was no hypocrisy, it being that which was natural to her, "we've just called to see you. We want a talk with you very particularly. Shall we come in, or would you rather come somewhere and have dinner with us?"

The girl looked frightened, reluctant, almost sullen, as she replied defensively: "What's it about?"

"I don't want to begin in the street. But it won't take long if we can get somewhere where we can feel we shall be alone."

"It's not anything about Mr. Ames, is it?"

"I'd rather not talk in the street, if you don't mind."

The girl looked rebellious, but hesitant. She may have felt that there was no escape. Her mind may have gone back, inconsequent though it may seem, to that refusal of extra wages which she had heard two or three hours before, which was partly responsible for the bad temper she was certainly in. She said: "Well, that means it is. You can come in if you like, but you'll get nothing from me."

The hopes of her hearers rose as she said that. For was it not an admission that there was something to be got? Belle risked the whole position, while the door was still not opened to let them in, by saying: "Clara seemed to think differently."

The girl answered angrily: "So you've been at her? She'd no right to say that. Let her speak for herself." But as she said this, her latchkey was in the door, and she was leading the way to a back-room on the first floor, which they saw as they entered to be neater, tidier, and better furnished than would have been expected from the blowsy woman they had first seen, or the state of the dingy stairs.

Bessie said ungraciously: "You'd better sit down." She indicated the two vacant chairs that the room contained. She threw her hat and coat onto the bed. She put a match to the gas fire. She cleared a third chair for her own use.

Belle said: "May I smoke?" Receiving the expected consent, she offered her cigarette case to Bessie, which was not refused. Reggie took another. He produced a lighter. The atmosphere slightly thawed.

Miss Butcher was not normally a bad-tempered girl. She was recovering from the first effect of the unexpected encounter. There was weariness, but no hostility, in her voice as she asked: "Well, what is it you want to know?"

"We are very anxious to get at the truth about my Uncle's death. You can understand that. And we think you may be able to give us important help."

"Well, you're wrong there."

"Perhaps so. But we're willing to risk it. We don't want you to do it for nothing. We want to ask you three questions, and we'll give you five pounds for each answer."

As Belle spoke she drew three five-pound notes from her bag.

The girl looked at them with obvious interest, but said shrewdly: "You mean if you get the answers you want from me?"

As she said this, Reggie felt a doubt, which had been lurking before, as to whether the crudity of this method of bribery might not defeat itself. What might answers so bought be worth? But he had promised not to butt in, and Belle gave the right reply.

"I don't mean that at all. We want to get at the truth. We'll risk what it may be worth to us."

The girl still looked dubious. Was there a catch? Who was to decide whether she were telling the truth? But you can buy many attractive things for £15 in the Edgware Road. She said: "I'd like to know what the questions are."

Belle pulled out a slip of paper on which Reggie had typed copies of the three questions which Mr. Jellipot had suggested. She said: "They're quite easy. The first is only what can you tell us about Mr. Ames' hours at the office, and when, and which way, did he go home at night?"

Miss Butcher looked surprised. If the questions were all like that, she would never have earned £15 so easily in her life before!

"I'll tell you what I know about that," she said readily. "He used to come to the office first thing in the morning. My time's eight-thirty, but he used to be before me more mornings than not. Between nine and a quarter past, he used to go out to see Mr. Briggs, as we understood. Sometimes he'd have Miss Marchant in his room first, to give her some work to do.

"If that made him a bit late, he might have a taxi called, but mostly he went by bus—I've seen him get on it once or twice, and he used to come back the same way.

"He used to have lunch at the office at twelve o'clock. It was always sent in from the *Prince of Wales*. Then he went on working till two-thirty or three, and after that he often went out—seeing customers, I suppose—in the afternoon."

Reggie spoke for the first time. "Are most of the customers in London?"

"Yes. Or, at least, they have London offices. They're large electrical firms, or export merchants, most of them that matter."

"So," Belle asked, "it was a natural thing for him to do?"

"Yes. I suppose so. I never thought anything different."

"I don't see why anyone should. I suppose he brought orders back?"

"I don't know. Miss Marchant would know more about that."

"Well, go on. Did he come back at the end of the afternoon?"

"Not always. Not so often as not. Just enough to make us careful not to slip off too early."

"And when he did come back, how did he go home?"

"On the 111 bus, I suppose. I didn't see him get on, if you mean that."

"You just suppose he did, because it would be the natural thing for him to do?"

"Yes. I don't say I didn't see him get on once or twice."

"You know where he lived?"

"Yes. Everyone did."

"Could you tell me more about how he spent his time after office hours?"

"Not much. Clara'd know more about that."

Belle felt disinclined to press the question further. She looked interrogatively at Reggie, who said: "I think Miss Butcher has told you everything as accurately as she can." It did no more than confirm what he had learnt already from other sources. Neither of them knew why Mr. Jellipot attached importance to these movements.

Belle passed over one of the five-pound notes, and the girl took it quickly enough but with an exclamation as though excusing herself: "Well, if it's worth that to you!"

"The other questions are a lot simpler. You can answer them in about half a dozen words. The first one is: "Did he wear a wig?"

The question appeared to startle the girl. She stared: "How should I know?"

"Oh, you might! I suppose wigs sometimes fall off, or slip sideways."

Miss Butcher's face had changed. She seemed to be restraining a resentment she did not know how to express. She said with finality in her tone: "I think I'll give that question a miss."

"Then I don't think it would be any use asking you the third," Belle replied, with equal finality, putting the two remaining banknotes back into her bag. "Thank you for all you've told us."

Seeing that she was getting up to go, Reggie did the same. He felt that they were giving up rather too easily, but he could not debate that there.

When they were in the street, Belle said: "I'm sure she knows something she won't say. But we shouldn't have got it now. We should only have fallen out, which would be like banging the door.

"I wonder whether you'd better tell Mr. Jellipot what you've found out so far, and see whether he can make anything of it.

"If he thinks it's very important to find out what that young woman knows, I might get something if I should see her alone. She might tell me things that she wouldn't let out to you."

Reggie made no objection to that. His immediate concern was that they should go back to the Regent Street together, and that as long a time as possible should be spent in narrating to Muriel what had occurred.

CHAPTER XXII.

Miss Butcher Alters Her Mind

BESSIE arrived at the works somewhat later than usual, after a restless night, and almost immediately sought an interview with her employer.

She said: "Miss Reeves—Miss Arabella, I mean—came bothering me last night, with one of Mr. Jellipot's clerks. They wanted to know all sorts of things about Mr. Ames."

"It is a position," Mr. Gilson replied, without appearing particularly interested in the girl's statement, "in which such enquiries must be expected. I hope you were able to tell them what they wanted to know."

"They wanted to know if he wore a wig."

"Wore a wig?" Mr. Gilson appeared surprised. "Why should he? He appeared to me to have as much hair of his own as any reasonable man could require, if not more. Now, if they had asked why he didn't visit the barber more frequently!"

"Well, if he did, he hadn't."

"Yes. I see what you mean. That sounds reasonable. Were you able to gratify their curiosity?"

"I told them I'd got nothing to say. I wondered whether you'd thought over what I asked yesterday. About giving me a rise."

Mr. Gilson was giving her his full attention now. "Is there," he asked, "any reason why I should do so, which I might not have known yesterday?"

"Well, they offered me five pounds."

"Five pounds to say that Mr. Ames wore a wig? I should have thought Mr. Jellipot would have had more sense."

"Well, I didn't say anything."

"Which you wish me to take as a reason why I should advance your wages? Miss Butcher, you are employed here to pack parcels, and the idea that you can earn overtime money by stating that gentlemen do, or do not, wear wigs is a delusion which I am unable to encourage.

"I have no idea what you may mean, but I feel that it will be better in every way that you should look for employment elsewhere.

"But, as I am not likely to see you again, I will just give you one word of advice. Mr. Ames, whatever the future may hold, is not yet a convicted criminal. If he should reappear, I suppose that, from what has come to my own ears, he could bring enough actions for slander to obtain damages which would keep him in comfort for the rest of his life.

"You may think that, as you have little to lose, that does not matter to you—but there are criminal courts."

"You mean I'll get prosecuted if I say that Mr. Ames wore a wig?"

"No. I don't think you could. I doubt whether to say that a man wears a wig can be considered a slander at all. Now, if it were a woman—but it is a question for a lawyer rather than for me to answer."

"Well, I'm sorry if I've said anything wrong. I don't want to leave. I've got used to it here."

"I'm afraid it's too late to say that now."

Mr. Gilson touched his bell, and his new secretary appeared.

"I want you," he said, "to pay Miss Butcher a month's money in lieu of notice. She will be leaving in half an hour."

It was doubtless in consequence of this decisive interview, and of a certain impetuosity in the character of Bessie Butcher when roused to wrath, that Mr. Jellipot, while listening to Reggie Tudor's narrative of his amateur detective work, received this letter:

Dear Sir,

If you like to send someone again, there's one or two things I've remembered that you might like to know.

Yours truly,

Bessie Butcher

Mr. Jellipot read it with his usual care, and passed it over to Reggie, with the remark: "When this letter was brought in, I was on the point of saying that you appear to me to be on the right road, though you have not got far, and it may prove one which we cannot trace to any conclusive end.

"I am afraid I was also likely to have added some criticism upon—shall I say the directness?—of Miss Arabella's financial approach to Miss Butcher, and to regret that you had not continued your own more pedestrian methods. You may think this letter to be a substantial answer to such criticism. I am not sure. But it is a point on which we may all hope that I shall be proved wrong.

"Anyway, you will not mind the expenditure of time required for taking the note to Miss Arabella this evening. No? So I supposed. But I suggest that you should let her see Miss Butcher alone. If she can get the girl to talk freely, she may go beyond answering the specific questions you have in mind—perhaps beyond anything that we are able to guess."

With these words, Mr. Jellipot dismissed his clerk, and turned to the consideration of other matters, to be interrupted almost immediately by a phone call from Mr. Gilson. That gentleman said he had decided to sell the business. To sell it at once. Could Mr. Jellipot see him tomorrow morning to take his instructions?

"You mean, of course, the stamp business?" Mr. Jellipot queried.

"No. I'm meaning to keep that. I'm selling Briggs & Co. The business here."

"It is a somewhat sudden decision."

"Yes. I'll explain when I see you."

Mr. Jellipot consulted his diary. "Shall we say 10:45? Yes, if necessary, I can give you a clear hour."

He rang off. He said to himself, not for the first time, that it was the queerest affair he'd ever known. It was not long before that Gilson had said that he was selling the stamp business, and had changed his mind in a few hours. Now he had resolved, with the same appearance of precipitation, to sell the major business, which had become adequately capitalised, had passed entirely into his hands, and had every prospect of a successful future.

Well, there must be an explanation! But what could it be? And was it possible that it would throw light on the bedroom murder with which, on all the available evidence, Gilson had had nothing to do?

He would soon know.

CHAPTER XXIII.

Mr. Gilson Dislikes Mr. Ames

IT seemed improbable that there could be any connection between the revelations promised by Miss Butcher, whatever they might prove to be, and Mr. Gilson's decision to sell the business. They were too remote. And there was no evidence—and, on the information Mr. Jellipot then had, there was no apparent probability—that Gilson knew of the young woman's offer, or even that she had been approached. There was the coincidence of time, and no more.

Yet Mr. Jellipot, pondering during the night the possible significances of the information which Reggie Tudor had already obtained, found satisfaction in expecting that he would have the benefit of Miss Butcher's further statements before Mr. Gilson would appear.

It was in that anticipation, and a confidant judgment that where Arabella had been Reggie had not been distant, that he called him into his office that morning immediately on his own arrival.

But he found that there was very little to hear. Belle had gone alone, as he had advised, although Reggie had been no further away than the street corner, but she had found no occasion to stay. She had been told that Miss Butcher was out, and that she had left a message that if any of Mr. Jellipot's people should call, she would see them at ten-thirty the next morning. Actually, she had supposed that there would be little prospect, or none, that any callers would appear so promptly, for she had not expected her letter to be delivered before the morning.

Belle had gone again, to be there at the appointed time, and Mr. Jellipot could learn no more than was implicit in the presumption that Miss Butcher had left her employment with some abruptness, or she would not have been free until a much later hour.

"Well," he thought philosophically, "it is improbable that it will make any eventual difference. I must hear what Gilson has got to say."

Mr. Gilson came punctually. His demeanour was outwardly unperturbed, but Mr. Jellipot's keen though unobtrusive scrutiny led him to the conclusion that he was interviewing a worried man.

Mr. Gilson had a bluntness of speech which Mr. Jellipot approved. He began: "I expect you're surprised that I've decided to sell out. I don't mind telling you why, but I'll say at once that I've not come to discuss whether it would be a good thing to do. My mind's made up."

"Rather sudden, is it not?"

"Not so sudden as you may think."

"You made a similar decision regarding the stamp business, and then changed your mind."

"I changed my mind about that for the same sort of reason that's deciding me now."

Mr. Jellipot answered only with a tentative: "Yes?" Let him talk. It was improbable that he would say much without throwing some light on a mystery which did not lessen.

It was evident that that was no more than Gilson was willing to do.

"The fact is," he began, "I can't stand the way the business came into my hands."

"You mean through the murder of Mr. Briggs?"

"Yes. Through Ames."

"You have no doubt that he was the criminal?"

"No. It seems to me that anyone can see that."

"I am very much of the same opinion."

"I never liked Ames. I may have told you that before. But I thought that I could forget all that had happened and give the business a fresh start. Well, I find I was wrong. I'd rather go back to my old business, and my old life, and forget the whole thing."

"Finding a purchaser may be a matter of some time. You will carry on till that can be done?"

"Yes, of course. Or unless you could find me a good manager in the meantime."

"That might not be impossible. You must have conceived a strong aversion to the business? You spoke differently when I saw you last."

"Yes. I know. You'll think it's silly, but somehow there's the spirit of Ames all about the place. I can't explain it. And it isn't my feeling alone. There was a warehouse girl who left some weeks ago

90

without any sensible reason. She said something about seeing ghosts. And there was an episode of a rather different kind yesterday. I'm not acting because of that, but I think it was the last straw. There was another warehouse girl coming to me with a tale that she would give you information about Ames, unless I raised her wages. She may not have actually said that, but it came very near. Of course, I told her to say what she liked, and gave her the sack. She had a month's money, and went."

"You certainly took the right course. Blackmailing would be a lean profession if everyone should act with equal wisdom. But it is rather difficult to see why she should think that you would object to her giving information about Mr. Ames."

"No. I didn't understand that myself. I suppose the girl was half-baked. And she was too vague for me to call it actual blackmailing. But it's all part of an atmosphere that I don't like. As a matter of fact, I should say she probably may know a good deal about Ames, though it doesn't follow that it would be any use to the police.

"One of the most unpleasant things about him was that he seems to have had a use for that kind of girl. There was a typist I had to sack almost as soon as I took control."

Mr. Jellipot said with sincerity (for he was of a shy and fastidious temperament) that it was not easy to understand. He undertook that suitable advertisements of the business should be drafted during the afternoon, and read over to Mr. Gilson on the telephone for his approval. So the interview terminated, leaving the solicitor more puzzled than he had been previously.

The reason for selling the business seemed inadequate, and yet he could not advise himself that Gilson had been insincere. A solicitor has much practice in distinguishing between genuine and simulated feelings, and Mr. Jellipot could tell himself, without vanity, that he was rarely misled.

He thought also that Gilson's expressions of aversion for Ames were the product of genuine feeling. That he should feel repulsion toward one whom he regarded as the perpetrator of a cold-blooded murder was not, in itself, surprising. But to conform it with the theory of the crime which Mr. Jellipot, though shy of giving it utterance, had been cherishing inwardly with an increasing confidence, was very puzzling indeed. Well, he must wait to hear what Miss Arabella would have to say.

CHAPTER XXIV.

The Statement of Bessie Butcher

BELLE reached Mr. Jellipot's office just as he had concluded that she could not be coming before lunch, and was taking his umbrella out of the stand.

"You have, perhaps," he asked, "a good deal to tell me?"

"I've got some surprising things, if they're true, as I think they are. At least, they were surprising to me, but I expect you'll say that you knew them, more or less, or you wouldn't have written down what you did."

"I am unlikely to say that I know anything. The case baffles me completely. But perhaps you will join me at lunch, and you can tell me what you have heard without my losing more time during an exceptionally busy day. And, if you don't mind, we'll have Reggie with us. It's due to him to hear what you've got to report."

Belle said yes to that. She looked pleased. Mr. Jellipot thought: "That young man's getting on;" and then reminded himself of his conviction of the sincerity of Gilson's dislike for Ames, and of the enigma it raised—if it were true. Had his powers of observation become unreliable? Was he suffering from premature senile decay?

Reggie showing no disinclination to join the little party, Mr. Jellipot led the way to Bentley's, and having ordered a lunch such as was only possible in those pre-ration days, he asked Belle to tell him what Miss Butcher had told to her.

"She had a row with Mr. Gilson yesterday morning, and she got sacked. She wasn't very clear as to what it was about, but it seemed as though she thought that if she didn't take our money for talking, he ought to give her something for keeping quiet. But why should he? When I asked her that, I couldn't get an answer that made sense.

"But she was quite willing to talk, so long as it didn't mean her having to give evidence in a court, and I told her I didn't see how it

92

could. What she's telling us may help the police to catch Ames, but when that's done they wouldn't have any more interest in her.

"I don't think she knows anything about the murder more than we all do. And, if she does, she hasn't given me any hint.

"But she says that both Clara and she went to his flat at night— she wouldn't say how many times, but she wanted me to think that it was more Clara than she, which may be true.

"She says that Clara told her she knew that he wore a wig. She couldn't say she knew it herself for a fact, but she had no doubt it was true.

"How you came to guess it, I can't imagine. But you guessed right.

"And it was just the same with the third question. She said they both knew that. He wasn't a fat man. He was thin. For some reason he stuffed his clothes."

"So she earned the money you offered?"

"Yes, she's had the ten pounds."

"Which doesn't exactly increase the value of what she said?"

"I don't see that. I told her we only wanted the truth. I should have paid her just the same if she'd said he was as fat as a prize pig. Besides, they're not things you want her to swear to. They must be to help you to catch Ames, and if you do, you'll find out for yourselves, without asking her."

"That," Mr. Jellipot conceded, "is a logical argument, and I have to thank you for what you have done, and for the substantial expenditure which you have made. You may conclude, not unreasonably, that, as my guesses were right, they must go very far towards substantiating the theory on which they were based, however fantastic at the time I may have felt it to be.

"But it is curious that, on the very day on which you bring me this confirmatory evidence, I have seen reason of a less material kind to think that it may not be true.

"And that, by a train of thought which I need not explain, brings me to another matter which it may interest you to hear. Mr. Gilson wishes to sell Briggs & Co. He wishes to sever his connection with it absolutely, and as soon as it can possibly be arranged."

Belle exclaimed: "But I thought he...." Surprise seemed to be too great for its more complete expression.

"So we may all have done. But those are his instructions to me today, and I do not think they will be changed."

Belle asked: "How much does he want?"

"A final figure has not been fixed." Mr. Jellipot smiled. "Am I to understand that you are a possible purchaser?"

"I should like to let Uncle Phillip know."

"If Sir Phillip should be disposed to negotiate, you will understand that I am acting for Mr. Gilson, and that he should have separate legal advice."

"Oh, you don't know Uncle! He's quite able to look after himself, and me too. But I don't want Uncle Adrian's business to be sold without our having a look in."

"Mr. Gilson will probably be glad to come to any reasonable terms with you or your uncle. He expressed anxiety to sell at an early date. I will enquire his price, and let you know. But you have gained information about Ames today which I think the police should have. I think they should also know to whom they will owe the credit of its acquisition. I have a very busy afternoon, but my evening is free. Suppose we meet at your hotel—you will be my guests for dinner, of course—and I ask Inspector Combridge to join us there?"

Belle said that would be delightful, and Reggie (who had found himself somewhat excluded from the conversation, and had occupied his time mainly in admiration of the young lady's profile as it was turned in Mr. Jellipot's direction), replied "Rather," when asked if it would be convenient to him.

Mr. Jellipot went back to his office, having formed a sound opinion that Reggie would be able to accompany Miss Arabella to the nearest bus without his assistance. He had a busy time, as he had forecast, but he telephoned Mr. Gilson, and obtained his consent to delay the advertisements for a few days, in view of the fact that he was already in touch with a possible buyer, which saved him some work, and his managing clerk more; and having disposed of that, he rang up Scotland Yard, and was fortunate in getting Inspector Combridge promptly.

"I have information about Ames," he said, "which you ought to know."

"Well—if it's important," came the reply in a voice of resignation. "I'm up to the neck now in the Borthwick case. I suppose tomorrow'll do? Unless you can let me have it over the phone."

"I want to ask you first whether you took any fingerprints, particularly those of Ames?"

"There weren't any in the bedroom which were any use to us, if you mean that."

"Not precisely. In a word, have you got Ames' fingerprint or do you know of any way in which they could be obtained?"

"No. How should we? I've told you there were none in the bedroom. The razor, together with what we thought were an unusual number of other things, must have been carefully wiped. But you know that most of the contents of a bedroom are soft, and don't take them. And the rest get them wiped off every day. In any case, Ames' prints, except on the razor itself, would have been no use to us. We knew he'd been there. That was an admitted fact. We've got Gilson's, though that's something he doesn't know. Not that they've been any use to us."

"You've got Gilson's, but not Ames'? I'm afraid there's no help in that."

"What use did you think they'd be?"

"I can't explain it all over the phone, and tomorrow won't be convenient for me. But I've got information that you'll prefer to have direct rather than it should reach your department in other ways. I suppose you never thought that Ames might be wearing a wig?"

"You mean he's shaved his hair off? And that's how he's been evading us? Then you must know where he is."

"I'll tell you if you'll join a little party for dinner at the Regent Street Hotel at seven-thirty tonight."

There was a moment's silence, and then a voice which indicated no pleasure at the prospect said: "Yes, I'll be there."

After that Mr. Jellipot phoned the hotel, and arranged for the projected dinner to be served in the Misses Reeves' private suite. As he did so, he became aware that Muriel must be present. He had overlooked that. But it was too late to make any alteration now.

CHAPTER XXV.

MR. JELLIPOT'S THEORY

"I SUPPOSE," Inspector Combridge began, with a natural misunderstanding, "that you knew all along that Mr. Tudor was on to something juicy, but you wanted to dish it up in your own way?"

Mr. Jellipot remembered his previous reticence. Reggie had not been on to anything juicy at that time, unless the young lady who was now sitting between them could be so described, and that was a suggestion which might not have been well received, and which, in any case, was a kind of joke which was unlikely to pass the solicitor's circumspect lips. He said: "Mr. Tudor wasn't after anything whatever connected with this case when you were interested in him previously; but enquiries which our young friends have recently been making at my suggestion have resulted in some interesting facts being discovered this morning, which they are here to pass over to you without delay."

"You see," Muriel said quietly, "our uncle was murdered, and we wanted the matter properly cleared up."

Inspector Combridge felt vaguely that he had been rebuked, without being clear as to his fault. He said: "Of course, I understand that. We're always grateful for any help we can get. If you can tell me how to put a hand on Robert Ames...."

"We can't tell you that," Belle replied. "But we can tell you that you've been looking for the wrong kind of man. You've been asking the whole country to look out for a fat, red-headed man, and Mr. Ames happens to be bald and thin."

The inspector looked puzzled, and then sceptical. "You're not going to tell me that he disguised himself before he committed the crime? And how long before would it have been?"

"That," Mr. Jellipot said, "is what appears to have been the position, however improbable it may sound. The fact is that there are two young women who are, or rather were, employed by Briggs &

Co., who admit that they were on sufficiently familiar terms with Ames to visit him at his flat, and whose combined evidence is that he wore a wig, and stuffed out his clothes to give him an appearance of corpulence."

"You think this isn't a sell?"

"I feel some confidence that it is true."

"It's queer, with all the enquiries we made, that we heard nothing of this."

"Perhaps you didn't ask."

"Well, who would? Besides, we don't ask leading questions like that. If we did, we should get told a lot more lies than we do now."

"Mr. Jellipot," Belle said, "wrote down the questions, just as though he knew what the answers were going to be."

"I think," Mr. Jellipot said, "that a position has developed that makes it necessary that I should tell you what had gone on in my mind, however foolish you may think it to be. But I should add that just as this evidence, which has the appearance of confirmation, comes, I have reason, on quite other grounds, to think that I may be wrong. A small matter, which it would be useless to mention now, caused the perverse idea to enter my mind that Ames and Gilson might be the same man. I should add that I propose to put this to Mr. Gilson tomorrow, and I quite anticipate that it may end in my apologising to him for having had such a foolish thought."

There was a moment of silence. The inspector had a look of incredulity as his trained mind went over all the difficulties—were they not impossibilities?—that this theory involved.

Reggie sat in silent expectation of what would follow. He had a respect for Mr. Jellipot which was reluctant to accept the probability that he had been wrong, even from his own lips. But it did take some swallowing! You couldn't deny that.

Belle said: "Why, of course! That explains everything. I wonder we didn't think of it before."

Muriel said: "Oh, Belle! I don't think you should say that. Even Mr. Jellipot isn't sure."

They were interrupted by the serving of dinner, which gave each of them an opportunity of assimilating this surprising theory before further discussion became possible, which, if it brought no wisdom, may have checked the saying of some foolish things.

CHAPTER XXVI.

MR. JELLIPOT DEFENDS HIS THEORY

WHEN they were alone again, Inspector Combridge began: "I don't see how...," and Mr. Jellipot interrupted with: "I think it may save time, and perhaps be fairest to myself, if I tell you how my mind worked, and how I developed a theory at which I must expect you to laugh, unless it should prove true, which I do not claim it to be.

"I observed, on first consideration, a number of supporting details, which led me to the decision that it could not be dismissed without conclusive probing.

"How had Gilson first come on the scene? In answer to an advertisement which Ames had proposed. Obviously he could answer his own advertisement. How had he been selected? Ames had interviewed other enquirers, and had given them accounts of the business which had led them to withdraw.

"Ames had been, at that time, under some measure of suspicion, as one who might be responsible, either by mismanagement or dishonesty, for the difficulties into which the business had fallen. I confess that I did not trust him, but I had thought that an incoming partner would have made a sufficiently stringent investigation, either personally or through professional agents, to exonerate or convict him, and I was proportionately reassured when Mr. Gilson said that he had satisfied himself of Mr. Ames' probity, and had sufficient confidence in him in other ways to agree that he should continue to manage the business.

"It is evident that this is just what would have occurred had the two men been one, and, had there been irregularities of whatever kind, it might have been possible to cover them in no other way.

"If we premise that such irregularities had occurred—if, for instance, Ames had misappropriated monies which he had invested in the name of what I may call his alternative personality—it would be the one way in which he could bring the needed money back into the business under his own control, and at the same time bury his defalcations beyond any probable discovery.

"To then get rid of Briggs, and of the now redundant Ames, would be a final stroke by which he would complete possession of the business, and remove a complication which would become increasingly difficult to sustain.

"It was a theory which supplied motives, the apparent absence of which was one of the greatest difficulties in attempting to solve the crime.

"Against these plausibilities there were manifest objections, and there was an almost certainty that, if it were not true, its impossibility would appear even upon cursory examination.

"For instance, it would have been so if I could have learned that Mr. Briggs had, at any time, met the two men together, or if they had met (as would have been most natural) at my office. But I could not discover that Briggs had ever seen them at the same time, and I remembered an occasion when I have asked them to see me, and Ames had failed to keep the appointment.

"I had understood, and had no reason to doubt, that Ames had met Gilson on several occasions at the works when the investigation of the business was proceeding. I had heard accounts, both from Gilson and Ames, of these interviews. But this again was no evidence, if my theory were true.

"These were supporting facts, but they were of a negative character. At the most, they showed that a monstrously improbable thing might have occurred, which fell far short of proving that it had.

"In addition, there was the extreme difficulty of explaining how one man could appear as two, particularly to Mr. Briggs and myself, without his identity being suspected. Some measure of disguise—of extremely clever disguise—there must surely have been. And here it was immediately evident that, if either were disguised, it must have been not Gilson, but Ames.

"A bald man may wear a wig, but one with a good head of hair cannot appear bald on alternate days. A thin man may increase his apparent bulk, but a fat one cannot make himself periodically thin.

"It followed that, if Ames had a head of genuine hair, or if his bulk were not artificial, there was an end to a most improbable theory. I was considering how I could arrive at a certain conclusion, and saw that a coroner's inquest, to which both men would be called as witnesses, would finally resolve it, but the inquest was adjourned, and after that the sudden disappearance of Ames increased my difficulty.

"I considered then that, if he were found, and came into the hands of the police—as he certainly would—such disguises would almost certainly be discovered, and a disclosure of the truth, with or without my assistance, would follow.

"On the other hand, were I wrong, I should have avoided exposing what I still regard as a theory of overwhelming improbability.

"If, however, he were not found, that theory would receive a little further support, though still of no more than a negative kind.

"As we know, all enquiries have failed, as, in a case of the kind, they seldom do; and when Miss Arabella expressed a particular desire that the mystery should be solved, I suggested a line of enquiry which has brought us to where we are."

Inspector Combridge spoke doubtfully: "It wasn't only the hair, or the being fat. They were such different men. But it almost sounds as though there's something in it to me. I wish you'd tell us why you think it's wrong now."

"I was proposing to do that. I ought first to point out that the evidence which it is understood that one or both of these young women are prepared to give was in response to suggestive questions by me, and, beyond that, that Miss Arabella paid substantially for the replies she got. It is true that she made it clear that the money would be paid whatever the replies might be; but it is right that you should know this.

"My own difficulty is of a different kind. I was talking to Gilson this morning, and he expressed a dislike of Ames—he has done that in previous conversations—which I could not doubt to be genuine, and which appeared to me to be radically inconsistent with the theory which I had formed.

"It goes even further than that. I have met Gilson several times, and he has always seemed to me to be of a standard of rectitude which is inconsistent with the criminality which my theory imputes."

"He might have been just putting it on."

"I thought not. Even with the suspicion I held, I was convinced that, even apart from the probability that Ames may be a murderer, he regards him with an active dislike."

Muriel, who had been listening with a silent intentness, sometimes with a bending of puzzled brows, but with no other sign of emotion, now spoke in a tone of quiet conviction, that had its influence on her companions: "It does sound queer, but I'm almost sure that you're right now. Mr. Gilson isn't that sort at all."

Perhaps Inspector Combridge was the least impressed. He was never easily to be influenced by what men said or professed. He would have said that he had heard too many lies, including some that were most expertly told. He sought facts. And it seemed to him that Mr. Jellipot had marshalled an impressive total. "You might give me the address of these young women," he said. "If they can make me believe their tale, I'll have Gilson where he belongs in the next hour."

"Then," Mr. Jellipot said, "you will be taking a very hazardous course. And you must please avoid saying that it was suggested by me."

"Because Gilson's convinced you that he's too good a man? Of course, that's what he set out to do as soon as he knew that those young women would be likely to blow the gaff. It's just window-dressing, if you ask me."

"But I do not regard it as hazardous on that ground alone. You will be charging a man almost entirely without evidence, or, at any rate, without such as any probable jury would accept."

"I don't see that. It seems to me to be about as good a case as I ever had."

"So it might to me if I had not considered it more thoroughly than you have yet had an opportunity to do.

"You must remember that you cannot charge Gilson with being Ames, which would not, in itself, be a criminal matter. You must charge him with the murder of Briggs."

"Well, if they're the same man...."

"You mean that their identity becomes an issue which you can raise? You are almost certainly right in that. But what evidence have you?

"You can put the two young women into the box, and their witness may be torn to shreds, or remain whole. But, if it survives cross-examination (and the probability is that it will be in a very damaged condition), how far have you got?

"You will have proved that Ames disguised himself. But that does not show that he was Gilson, any more (I will say) than you are me—but any bald-headed man who is of thin or medium build. Get Bulfit against you, and you could bet on an acquittal before the prosecution would have begun."

Inspector Combridge looked unconvinced. "It seems to me," he said, "that we should have a good start, and most cases get a lot easier as you work them up."

CHAPTER XXVII.

SUPERINTENDENT ROOMER SAYS NO

SUPERINTENDENT ROOMER had heard many improbable tales, but nothing which he could recall as outrageous to credibility as that which Inspector Combridge had told him now.

So he said. But he added that Mr. Jellipot had the reputation of being an astute man, and, anyway, it was his theory, not theirs. It was the obvious course to interview the young women, and reconsider the position in the light of such statements as could be obtained from them.

Inspector Combridge recognized the official attitude of a dull man who played for safety first, but who would be sorry to miss the credit of such an arrest as might live for centuries, an unrivalled incident in the records of the C.I.D.

But there was a request which, as he had thought the matter over during the night, had seemed to him imperatively necessary to make to Mr. Jellipot before he should see Gilson again, and he wished to have behind it a higher authority than his own, for he had a doubt of whether the solicitor would give way to him.

"There's one matter that's rather urgent," he said. "If we don't stop Mr. Jellipot, he's intending to ask Gilson straight out whether he's Ames or not. Of course, he won't admit it. He'd be a mug if he did. But it's just putting him on his guard, which is about the last thing we ought to do."

"You mean you want us to phone Jellipot to say nothing?"

"Yes. If you could get the A.C. to make it a message from him, Jellipot might listen."

The superintendent looked doubtful.

"I don't think we should interfere."

"But surely...."

"Don't you think that Gilson's on his guard already? What about what that girl must have said to him before he sacked her?"

"That's the most puzzling thing of all, if he really is Ames. You'd think he'd have kept her sweet, whatever it cost. Sacking her the way he did is just asking for what he'll get."

"I don't know," the superintendent, who was by no means a fool, replied thoughtfully.

"We may find he's given us a hard nut to crack. Think what Bulfit might make of it, if he got the kind of jury he likes. Obvious action of an innocent man, and anything the young women say is just spite. He might say it was all invention from first to last. Or, if Ames *did* wear a wig, that they'd just used it to threaten Gilson, thinking he might be frightened enough to buy them off. Perhaps he'd suggest that the whole trouble came because Gilson wouldn't have the goings-on with them that Ames must have done. And couldn't he make out that that just proves that Gilson isn't the same man?"

"That's what Jellipot says is his difficulty. He says he doesn't behave like the same man. I told him it just showed what a clever rascal we should have the pleasure of running in."

"Perhaps it does, but it all sounds as though this isn't going to be an easy business for us. I'm sure of one thing. We'd better leave Jellipot to go his own way. He may get something that will smooth it all out. Or if he says he's sure it's not the same man, we may be very glad that we haven't interfered."

Inspector Combridge, though not entirely convinced, gave way before this attitude of his superior officer.

He remembered that Mr. Jellipot had expressed doubt of whether it would be an easy prosecution. He saw that Superintendent Roomer's official caution was becoming alive to the same danger. Though he was more capable of taking a risk which his instinct of duty might require, he was not himself insensible to such considerations.

So far he had done nothing more than report the solicitor's surprising theory, and the arguments with which he had supported it. Now he was going to interview the two young women, and, if possible, get written statements from them. Doing that, he was on safe ground. But the idea of the hasty arrest of Gilson had somewhat receded in his mind as this conversation proceeded.

Anyhow, let Jellipot try his own line, without being able to say afterwards that he had been hindered by any request from them.

CHAPTER XXVIII.

MR. GILSON DISCUSSES MR. AMES

MR. JELLIPOT said: "There is a possibility—I ought not to use a stronger word—that members of the Reeves family may be prepared to relieve you of your interest in Briggs & Co., provided, of course, that your wish to dispose of the business remains unchanged, and that a price can be agreed. I have told them that I cannot act for both parties, and that they should seek other advice."

Mr. Gilson looked pleased. He said: "That would be more than satisfactory to me. But it is not a position in which you need hesitate to act for them. I shall be quite prepared to accept any price which you approve, and which they are willing to pay."

"That is generously said, but I am still not sure that I can alter my decision. I suppose you would be willing to continue to manage the business until a satisfactory substitute could be found?"

"I should prefer not to make any pledge of that kind. My wish is to sever my connection with it as promptly as is any way possible."

"You must have a very strong feeling upon that point. Is it permissible to ask whether the trouble you have had with one or more of the staff has anything to do with your decision?"

"It is a natural question. If I reply frankly, I must say that it has, but I cannot say how much. I may say that everything has been pushing me in the same direction."

"May I ask whether either of the young women went so far as to attempt to identify you with Robert Ames?"

A look of surprise came to Mr. Gilson's face at this question, and whether it were genuine or not, Mr. Jellipot owned to himself that he could not tell.

"No. How should they? I don't say that some such allegation may not have been implied in Miss Butcher's attitude. But, if she meant to say it, she didn't get as far as she had intended. I cut her short with a month's money. But I expect you've heard about that.

And it's an easy guess that you know more than I do about what the young woman is saying now. Not that it matters to me. If anyone listens to blackmailers, they don't deserve any sympathy if they find they've been led up the garden path."

"Perhaps not. But I will be at least as frank with you as you are with me. There was a time when the idea that you and Ames might be the same man—however fantastic it may sound—did enter my own mind."

"I should have thought anyone could have seen the difference at the first glance. May I ask why?"

"Yes. It was before the murder. When you came in to sign the partnership deed, you had gloves on, though it was not a cold day. When you signed, you drew off (at my suggestion) the right glove. As you did so, I noticed an unhealed cut at the inside junction of the second and third fingers, and I remembered that there had been a similar one on the hand of Robert Ames on the previous day. It is not a place which is frequently cut, and the coincidence intrigued my mind."

"I remember that. It was a simple accident. A knife slipped when I was engaged upon a rather delicate operation upon a stamp of some value. All the same, I am not Robert Ames, and I should find it difficult to believe that such a proposition would be seriously considered by the police. But, if it were, may I ask whether I could rely on you to act for me?"

Mr. Jellipot pondered this, and then answered with deliberation: "No. I don't think you could."

"You don't seriously think that I am Ames?"

"I have a singularly open mind."

"Then I can respect your attitude. You would not care to defend one who might have been guilty of a crime of such atrocity. But I will not only repeat that I am not Ames, I will add that, on the hypothesis which you have put before me, you might be unjust.

"Most men have capacities both for good and evil. Suppose a man *should*—it is your proposition, not mine—live two separate lives which, perhaps by deliberate intention at first, and then by the natural development of those beginnings, should become diverse in thought and character as well as in occupation. Suppose, to come more nearly to the present subject, that the one—shall we say the inferior?—personality should commit a crime for the benefit of the other, which that other should loathe and regret, and of which he would have been absolutely incapable in the hours of his own existence. Would it be just for him, in that personality, to bear the penalty of the crime?"

Mr. Gilson had spoken up to this point in a tone of earnestness such as led Mr. Jellipot to wonder whether it were not a personal problem which he had put forward in this abstract form, but now he changed to a lighter note as he concluded: "You may consider it too fantastic an idea to be worthy of serious question, but it is one which your own no less fantastic suggestion has raised; and I think you have the type of mind by which such problems are entertained."

"It is certainly a curious proposition," Mr. Jellipot conceded, "but do you think the degree of deviation…?"

"You will not overlook the fact that if two persons begin to step in different directions, even though the first deviation be almost unnoticeable, every further step will increase their distance, until they pass from each other's sight."

"You seem to have given the problem some consideration."

"Is it not natural, when there are evidently some who would cast me for the part?"

"Perhaps it is. But you are suggesting a line of defence which could only be developed if you were to admit your identity with Robert Ames."

"Which I certainly cannot do. But I was not intending to suggest a line of defence. I anticipate no attack. I was discussing an abstract proposition concerning a hypothesis which appears to have arisen in other minds, without its implications having been fully seen."

Mr. Gilson left with few further words, having given Mr. Jellipot food for reflection such as was to keep him awake in the night hours, and to bring him to no certain conclusions.

For the dawn was near when he muttered more than once: "It is too much for me," but whether he alluded to the question of the identity of the two men, or, if they were one, whether it could be demonstrated by legal process, or whether his mind had been occupied with the problem of moral responsibility which Gilson had raised, did not appear.

CHAPTER XXIX.

Two Statements

"I HAVE seen the three young women," Inspector Combridge reported, "and the one who might have made the best witness—I mean Miss Marchant—is no use to us. The idea that Ames and Gilson are the same man had never entered her mind. I feel sure of that, and I daren't suggest it to her, for fear the other side should get hold of her, if we ever get as far as a prosecution, and make out that we'd been putting the idea into their heads. What's been done already goes too far in that direction for me, but I've got statements from the other two which seem to show that we ought to be looking for a lean bald-headed man, if they go no further than that."

As he spoke, he passed over the two statements, which Superintendent Roomer read aloud. The first was that of Bessie Butcher. After the usual preliminaries it went on: "I have been employed as a warehouse girl for nearly three years by Briggs & Co., electrical appliance manufacturers, of Kilburn, London, N.W.6, and the course of my work brought me into frequent contact with Mr. Robert Ames, who was the manager of the business during the whole of that period.

"On more than one occasion I visited him during the evening at the flat where he lived. I had opportunities to observe, and did observe, that though he had the appearance of a stout man, he was actually rather thin, his rotundity being caused by padding or stuffing within his clothes.

"I have already stated this to Miss Arabella Reeves, who gave me a five-pound note for the information, but she did not pay me to say so. She said that she would give me the money if I would reply to her question, whatever the answer might be.

"She also asked me whether Robert Ames wore a wig, and I told her that I could not say so certainly from my own observation, though I believed it to be the case. I told her that Miss Clara Shole,

107

who was employed with me in the warehouse, had told me that she knew it to be so. Miss Reeves also gave me five pounds for this reply.

"On a previous occasion Miss Reeves, who was then accompanied by Mr. Reginald Tudor, had seen me, and I had given them information concerning Robert Ames' daily habits, for which they had paid me another five pounds, but, on that occasion, I declined to answer the other questions, although the money was offered.

"The fifteen pounds which I have received in all from Miss Reeves induced me to answer the questions, which I was otherwise reluctant to do, but did not influence the nature of my replies in any way.

"After my first interview with Mr. Tudor and Miss Reeves above-mentioned, I reported what had occurred to the new manager of the business, Mr. Henry Gilson, who dismissed me at once, giving me a month's money in lieu of notice. I do not know why he should have done this. I then wrote to Mr. Jellipot to say that I would tell anything I knew, and Miss Reeves saw me as above-mentioned, on the morning following."

Miss Shole's statement said: "The statement of Miss Elizabeth Butcher dated the 17th of October, 1930, has been read over to me, and, so far as it relates to the physical appearance of Robert Ames, I agree with what it contains, which is within my own knowledge. I know that he was bald-headed and wore a wig, as there was an occasion when I saw it come off. I also know that his clothes were stuffed and padded. I left Briggs and Co. at my own desire, because it was so creepy. I did not think that Mr. Gilson was Robert Ames, as he was so different in his manners and the way he spoke, but I kept being reminded of Ames in ways that I didn't like."

These statements were, of course, not in the wording of those who signed them. It may be doubted whether Miss Butcher knew what rotundity meant, and she would certainly not have talked about "the morning following." But, apart from their police jargon (and that was not much), they were the result of an honest effort on the part of Inspector Combridge to set down what he understood that the young women were trying to say, as he considered they ought to say it.

Superintendent Roomer finished what he would have called their perusal, and said: "We've got more than a bit there. Especially from Clara Shole. What sort is she?"

"She's not the sort who makes a good witness. Since she left Briggs & Co. she's been helping an uncle who keeps the Turk's

Head in Kilburn High Road. She can tip up a glass herself, and I should say there isn't much of the wrong sort that she doesn't know.

"From something she let out, I got the idea that Ames had to turn her out when she wasn't finding it easy to walk straight, and they had a tussle, and she caught at his wig, and it came off in her hand."

"I see. She might not be a very creditable witness, but she might be particularly convincing, especially if she thought that the ordeal of the witness box required some alcoholic preparation. That part of her statement about the creepiness of being with Gilson is the best thing you've got. If she'd only go a step further, and say Gilson's Ames! She must know, one way or other, having been so familiar with Ames as she obviously was, and having seen him without his wig."

"So you'd think. But she won't say one way or other. So far, we've got no one who will. And without that—"

"Yes. That's the snag. I wish we could dress Gilson in red wig, and pad out his clothes, but I'm afraid—"

"No. We couldn't do that. And even that mightn't get us home. It isn't only the size and the wig. There's more difference; and if it's makeup, it's the cleverest thing I've ever seen. I've seen enough of the two men (if there were two) to understand that. Even Jellipot doesn't say that he can identify them himself as the same man."

"Well, we will hear what he has to say on that matter himself. When I heard that you were bringing in these statements, I asked him if he could spare the time for a conference, and I've sent a car for him. He might be here any minute now."

CHAPTER XXX.

TOO MUCH FOR MR. JELLIPOT

MR. JELLIPOT said: "Gilson denied being Ames, though he came near to admitting it when he argued that if he were, his moral responsibility for the murder, in his personality as Gilson, might not be great."

Superintendent Roomer was amused. "How did he make that out?" he asked.

"It is a theory," Mr. Jellipot replied, with his usual logical discrimination, "which many people would decline to take seriously.

"To do it what you may think to be more justice than it deserves, I may put it in this way: suppose that a man should, over a long period, live dual lives in which, by a deliberate preliminary decision, he should develop different habits and characteristics. That is what, if we entertain the hypothesis that Ames and Gilson are the same man, Ames (or Gilson) must have done.

"In the course of years Ames becomes or remains a bustling untidy, unmethodical man, while Gilson is deliberate, neat, and orderly. The difference in character and habits becomes so great that the very lines of his face change as he makes his daily transition.

"The moral differences are equally great. Gilson is reserved and fastidious. He does not merely abstain from unsavoury feminine companionships: they would be repugnant to him. But they are a natural relaxation to Ames.

"Ames was or becomes a man of unscrupulous ambitions and greed. He robs his trusting employer, and then, to avert discovery and retain his plunder, conceives the idea (or he may have had it from the first) of introducing Gilson as a partner in the firm, who will invest money made in the stamp business, or perhaps that of which Ames had been robbing the firm, or both.

"As Gilson, he stipulates cautiously that Briggs shall insure his life, and then, as Ames (in which personality he has already resolved

110

to disappear) he sees the opportunity of enrichment, and of getting complete control of the business, which murder will provide.

"This murder, perhaps by a sudden evil impulse, he commits. The event takes the course which he foresaw. The business becomes his as Gilson, while he disappears as the suspected Ames.

"Feeling secure, he resolves to sell the stamp business, and concentrate on his new possession.

"But he is already uneasy. In the atmosphere of the business which he had so long controlled in his character as Ames, he finds that he is developing an alarming tendency in unguarded moments to act and speak and even think as Ames, rather than as Gilson had been used to do.

"When Clara Shole leaves, hinting at 'ghosts,' he feels it to be a danger signal he must not disregard. To be Gilson for the whole twenty-four hours would, under any circumstances, have been difficult, but in that environment it is impossible. He cancels his advertisement of the stamp business, seeing that that background to the Gilson personality must be maintained.

"When Bessie Butcher blackmails him, he sees the danger signal more clearly still. He decides to cut his connection absolutely with Briggs & Co., and to give his entire time to the stamp business, to which his Gilson personality was naturally attached.

"Being policemen, you will (you must forgive me saying) instinctively conclude that this decision would be taken through fear of the law, but you might not be more than partially right. As Gilson, he may have had a genuine dislike for the Ames personality—even a man with no such duality of existence may despise himself for the sins of his weaker hours. He may have felt it intolerable that he should sink to be a perpetual Ames, even with the reward that Ames had sinned so deeply to get.

"Actually, whether or not Gilson be Ames, I think that he is sufficiently confident that it cannot be proved to feel almost indifferent to that aspect of the matter."

Inspector Combridge had been looking increasingly uncomfortable as Mr. Jellipot propounded this curious thesis. As it concluded, he said: "I suppose you're going to tell us now to lay off him, or you'll defend him on those lines, and make us look fools, as you did once before."

"I will not deny," Mr. Jellipot replied, "that I have considered how such a brief could be drawn, and that I think it would be an easier as well as a more intriguing occupation than to draw one for the prosecution. But that is not saying that I should undertake it. On the contrary, I should decline."

Superintendent Roomer, somewhat gloomily ruminating over Mr. Jellipot's efforts of imagination, and tapping the desk with his pencil, in a way he had when thought was easier than decision, took no notice of this exchange. He said only: "So that's how you think it is."

"I am not aware," the solicitor replied, "that I have said anything to justify that conclusion. It is too much for me. But, if Gilson be Ames, I think it might be difficult, if not impossible, to obtain evidence which would be likely to secure conviction against a reasonably strong defence. You have to remember that it has to be proved that Ames murdered Briggs. Standing alone, I think, if you had Ames in his admitted person, the evidence is strong enough, but with the double doubt—"

"Yes," the superintendent agreed, with no access of cheerfulness, "that's how it looks to me."

It was Inspector Combridge's stubborn persistence upon the trail which caused him to ask: "You don't mind telling us what first put this idea of Gilson being Ames into your head?"

Mr. Jellipot delayed his reply for a moment, but then he said: "No. It is knowledge which, I think, however inconclusive in itself, you are entitled to have. At the time of the signing of certain documents in my office on succeeding days, I noticed what appeared to be an identical cut in an unusual position upon the hand, or hands, of the two men. I should add that Gilson, who was my second visitor, wore a glove which he might not have drawn off had I not asked him to do so."

As they heard this, the two police officers looked at one another, and their eyes held the same conclusion, to which Roomer gave first expression.

"He's Ames right enough. The question is how we're going to bring it home. Sir Henry'll have to hear about this."

He still looked worried. It was the sort of case that careful detective officers wish to avoid: the sort that may do a man a lot of harm if it go wrong. An incalculable case. But if it should go right? There were attractive possibilities there.

CHAPTER XXXI.

BELLE SAYS THERE IS ONE WAY

SEVERAL weeks passed during which the only apparent consequence of what became known at Scotland Yard as the Jellipot
theory having been suggested to the police was that some thin bald-
headed men in different parts of the country, who, for various reasons, had not been long, or become well known, in the districts in
which they lived, were interviewed by the police, and required
(quite illegally) to prove to official satisfaction that they had been
similarly thin and bald at a date anterior to that on which Adrian
Briggs had died. One of these baited individuals, being of a regret-
tably irritable temper, had knocked down a detective sergeant, and a
discreet Home Secretary had insisted upon the incident being closed
without the publicity which a prosecution would have required.

Sir Phillip Reeves had come up from Cornwall, and Mr. Jellipot
had found him to be as tough and capable at a business deal as his
niece had indicated. He approved the purchase of the electrical business. He was active to discover, and judicious to select, a manager
who could take the place of the reluctant Gilson, and he settled
many details of the transfer direct with that gentleman, who met him
in so liberal a spirit that he was led to say to Mr. Jellipot that he was
as straight a man as he'd ever met.

"He has been," Mr. Jellipot replied, "of a disposition from the
first to close the deal, and to close it quickly."

"Well," Sir Phillip said, "after what he told me, I don't wonder
at that, though some men wouldn't be so sensitive when the pass-
book begins to talk. But it was a nasty business, and he told me that
he feels somehow responsible. He means that, if he hadn't come into
the business, things might have gone differently. I told him that was
a bit far-fetched, though I could see how he felt."

"It is not," Mr. Jellipot agreed, "a consequence of entering a
partnership which can reasonably be anticipated that a manager who

113

is maintained in his position will cut the throat of one of the parties concerned. I suppose that no sensible man would be disposed to blame Gilson for that."

"But there's a bit more in it," Sir Phillip went on. "He told me that there's a silly tale going about that he and Ames are the same man. I said I shouldn't let such cockeyed nonsense cost me a minute's sleep.

"But he stuck out that he didn't mean to leave it without an effort to make somebody sit up. He's advertising a £50 reward for information leading to the conviction of anyone who repeats the tale."

"That," Mr. Jellipot reflected, "is a most interesting development. But do I understand correctly that you had not heard that suggestion until it was mentioned by him?"

"No. I certainly hadn't. Do you mean that there are really people who take it seriously?"

"Yes. I may say there are. But my surprise arose from the fact that it had not been mentioned to you by your nieces. By Miss Arabella in particular."

"Well, she didn't. She told me that she wanted my opinion of Gilson before she'd say anything bad or good. I thought the way she said it was a bit queer, and I won't say that it didn't prejudice me against him at first, though I saw she'd tried to avoid giving that impression. But that soon wore off, and, if you ask me, I say he's a white man."

Mr. Jellipot said no more than that he was sure that both the young ladies would be interested to hear this opinion. He thought that the problem became more intriguing at each development.

He looked in the *Morning Post* next day, and found that Gilson had fulfilled his expressed intention, which Mr. Jellipot had doubted whether to take seriously.

He read:

> It having come to my knowledge that certain foolish or malicious persons are circulating a report that I am identical with one Robert Ames, whose present address is unknown, I hereby offer a reward of fifty pounds for information such as will lead to the conviction of any person repeating this criminal slander. Henry Gilson, Regent Street Hotel, W.1.

Mr. Jellipot's legal mind was not able to give entire approval to the wording of this advertisement, but he recognized that its intention and meaning were plain. He asked himself, did it indicate the indignation of an innocent, or the astuteness of a guilty man, and it was a question to which he found no certain reply.

Even of its astuteness, on the assumption that Gilson were Ames, he was less than sure.

He knew that the police were still undecided as to the course which they would pursue, and he judged that, in the absence of further evidence, it was improbable that they would venture to institute a prosecution. If they should do so, and the threat which the advertisement implied should remain unchallenged, Gilson's reputation would be largely cleared by the bold step he had taken. Should a prosecution be instituted, the fact that he had offered such a reward might be put to a jury in a way which would be favourable to him.

But that again was on the assumption that no one would accept the challenge which the advertisement gave. If they should, and Gilson should consequently be forced to prosecute, different considerations would arise.

So he said to Arabella, when she called with her sister to put their signatures to certain documents which the sale of the business required.

"Should he sue—he could not prosecute—anyone for such a slander, the jury's verdict might be as decisive as would be his own prosecution for murder by the police."

"Isn't it rather silly to talk about prosecuting, if he can't do it?" Belle queried.

"There is a legal distinction, of which he may not be aware. The only remedy for a spoken slander is a civil action. There must be written libel to enable the offended party to invoke the protection of the criminal courts."

"And then they'd get a chance of proving what they had said?"

"Even that might not be a complete legal defence. But—yes— that is substantially true."

"Then writing it would be the better way?"

Mr. Jellipot looked puzzled.

"If you mean worse for Mr. Gilson, you may be right. Written words cannot be disputed, and are supposed to be more deliberate. If they were of particular gravity, he might find himself almost driven to prosecute, which is a speedier process than a defended action in the civil court, and has other differences which might not be favourable to him.

"But that would be on the perhaps improbable assumption that a plea of justification would be entered by the one whom he would charge. It is more likely that there would be an attempt to obtain mitigation of penalty by apology and withdrawal. Indeed, it is not beyond the bounds of possibility—there have been precedents—that he might incite some unscrupulous individual to repeat the libel, under a bargain that it should be so withdrawn."

"You mean," Belle asked, "that he might pay someone to be prosecuted who would put up no defence?"

"He may have no such thought. But it has been done. Horatio Bottomley did it with temporary success."

"And after that the police would be more likely to let him alone?"

"If they had no evidence of collusion, it would be an additional reason why they would be reluctant to begin a hazardous prosecution."

"But if justification were pleaded, Mr. Gilson would have to come out of his shell?"

"That is an expression which is particularly apposite. The onus of proving justification would remain with the defendant but the prosecutor could be forced out of his shell."

"If this advertisement come to nothing, what are the police likely to do?"

"That, I believe, is still undecided. It is only yesterday that Inspector Combridge told me that the further enquiries he has been making have been entirely abortive."

"You said you wanted us to leave it to him."

"Yes. I felt that, after what you and Reggie had discovered, it had become a matter for the police. And it would have been a likely cause of confusion if you and they had continued parallel enquiries. But you must not assume that you would have succeeded where they have failed, even if failure be the right word to use."

"What have they been trying to find out?"

"It may have occurred to you that if we entertain the hypothesis that Ames and Gilson are the same man by whom your uncle was murdered, we are confronted with a particular difficulty. Ames, by the evidence both of the housekeeper and Mrs. Fishwick, left the house at about ten-thirty in the guise of Ames—an untidily-dressed redheaded man—and within twenty minutes, if not less, was calling at a house five minutes' walk away in the person and appearance of Gilson—his wig gone, the stuffing out of his clothes, those clothes almost certainly changed, and his whole aspect transformed.

"This has always seemed to me to furnish one of the strongest arguments against the theory of the identity of the two men. It only appears possible if we presume that Ames had some place of call approximately close to one of, or between the two, places at which the change could be made.

116

"Inspector Combridge tells me that he has made exhaustive enquiries without ascertaining that any house or room, furnished or unfurnished, was rented in either of the two names, or by anyone of corresponding appearance to either."

"And they're likely to do nothing because of that?"

"It is an argument in that scale."

"Then you see what a mess we're in?"

"The position is certainly complicated."

Muriel spoke for the first time: "We do really want to get the matter cleared up."

"We mean to do that," Arabella echoed, using a more emphatic word, though her voice lost nothing of its soft and musical quality, "and it seems to me there's only one way left."

"You can get Reggie to find out where Ames made the change, if that's what he did," Muriel suggested, with an implication which Inspector Combridge would not have appreciated.

"So we can. But I wasn't thinking of that."

With no further indication of what she meant, Arabella got up to go.

CHAPTER XXXII.

Should Belle Have Said That?

IT was during the evening of the same day that the Home Secretary almost collided with the Attorney-General as he was coming out of the Prime Minister's room. Sir Bulwer stopped abruptly.

"Oh, Danvers," he said, "you're just the man I was wanting to see. I've been over those papers you sent me in connection with the Briggs murder. Very interesting case. If you ask me, Gilson and whoever it was are the same man.

"But it's not the sort of dust you want to stir up unless you're quite sure that it won't settle in the wrong place.

"I've just been telling the P.M. about it, and he feels the same way. Make sure, he says, or do nothing at all. But if you are sure, it'll be a brief I shall like to have."

Mr. Danvers saw that the responsibility of final decision was to be left to him, and that he was to have no one to blame but himself if he came a cropper. He said: "Oh, well, I'm not intending to do anything without your advice."

Sir Bulwer could not object to that. What are Attorneys-General for? He said: "The case hangs too much on those two young women for me. And even if they were better witnesses than they are, they don't go far enough. If they'd say outright that Gilson is Ames, or even one of them..."

"One of them does."

"That's fresh. Which is it?"

"Clara Shole. We've heard that she's talking that way now in her uncle's bar."

"Oh, the one who knows how to lift her elbow? Well, there may be something in that. We'd better have another talk when we've both got more time."

They hurried into the House together, for the division bells were ringing.

It was true that Clara was becoming more definite in her assertions. She was talking freely, with her uncle's encouragement, for takings had risen since it had become known among Briggs & Co.'s workpeople that they could hear their employer denounced at the Turk's Head in so astounding a manner. And whether they were truth or a spiteful, half-drunken lie, Clara's words were to prove of decisive consequence, for it was owing to them that Mr. Gilson had inserted that challenging advertisement, as he had explained to Mr. Jellipot when he called, an hour after the young ladies had left, to contribute his own signature to the waiting documents.

"It's got to such a pitch," he said, "that I believe half the hands we employ think that I killed Briggs, and won't give me a civil word. It doesn't matter as much as it would if I weren't leaving, but, all the same, it's got to stop. If I let such talk go on, and do nothing, people—decent people, I mean—might get to think it was true. It might cling to me all my life. But if one of them gets into jail...."

"Yes. It is a course, both of reasoning and of action, which I am bound to approve."

"I'm glad to hear you say that, because, of course, if I do have to prosecute anybody, I shall want you to act for me."

"Which I should be obliged to decline. You must not overlook the fact that I have a measure of responsibility for what has occurred."

"Well, that's straight. But you're not responsible for these tales getting about. I don't suppose you've even seen Clara Shole, or the other girl, for that matter."

"No. I have not seen either of them."

"So I supposed. Well, I've given a fair warning, and the next one, man or woman, who says that I murdered Briggs, or that I'm that filthy Ames, which is almost as bad, will get what he or she ought to have."

"The whole matter," Mr. Jellipot responded, "certainly needs clearing up."

Mr. Gilson went on to his Strand office, to which he had become glad to escape from the atmosphere of the Kilburn works. He thought with satisfaction that, after next week, during which he had undertaken to initiate the new manager, he would be able to concentrate again upon a business which he wished he had never considered leaving.

He went on from there to the hotel, where he had dinner, as his custom was, in the public room. He did not expect to see anything of the Misses Reeves at that hour, knowing that they took the evening meal in their own suite, but, as he was giving his order to the waiter, he became aware that the two girls, with Reggie Tudor in close attendance, were crossing the room.

Their direct course from door to door would have left him somewhat aside, but Arabella, who was leading, turned toward him.

"I've got something to say to Mr. Gilson." Her voice, only slightly raised, was heard by a dozen surrounding diners.

She went on, as she reached his table, the others, who knew nothing of her intention, following closely: "I see you've offered a reward for anyone who'll tell you of someone else who says you are Robert Ames. Well, I'll save you that expense. I say you are Robert Ames, and I say you murdered my uncle. I can't put it plainer that that. I've written it here, so that there may be no mistake." She pulled a sheet of paper from her bag as she spoke, and laid it beside his plate.

Mr. Gilson looked at her quietly. "Is that all?" he asked, his lips smiling slightly, though his eyes were cold.

"It would be enough for most people."

"You are a very foolish young woman."

"Perhaps I am. But I shall tell everyone what I've said now, so you know what to expect. You can take it lying down if you like."

She went on to the door without waiting for a further reply. The diners at the surrounding tables had paused in astonishment at the dramatic challenge. Mr. Gilson, picking up his soup spoon, was the first to resume normality.

Muriel had been so astonished at her sister's action that she had not even uttered her frequent protest that Belle shouldn't have said that.

CHAPTER XXXIII.

MR. GILSON INSTRUCTS HIS LAWYERS

MR. GILSON considered a position he did not entirely like. He had been seriously resolved to stop the rumours which surrounded him in a growing volume. Inclination and reason had continued to urge him in that direction. But he had supposed that either his advertisement would be sufficient to put an end to talk which had become of such obvious danger, or that he would be able to prosecute some malicious or random gossiper who would find it difficult to engage a jury's sympathies, unless he could produce convincing evidence of the assertions which he had made.

Against such a defendant he was confident that he would prevail, and that a penalty would be inflicted such as would be his complete exoneration, and a sufficient deterrent to the wagging of other tongues.

He had not expected that he would be challenged to prosecute a girl of particularly attractive appearance, and the niece of the murdered man.

Yet such, it seemed, the course of events must be. He saw no tolerable path which avoided this, and when he went next morning to Messrs. Plumer, Plumer, & Plumer, to whom he had been urgently recommended by a legal acquaintance, he met with the same opinion.

Mr. Harold Plumer, Junior, who handled the most important items of the firm's extensive practice in the criminal courts, looking at Mr. Gilson's card, said: "Let Mr. Parks see him. No, I'll see him myself. Tell Mr. Parks to be ready if I want to pass him over to him."

But when he had listened for three minutes to Mr. Gilson's lucid account of his position, Mr. Harold rang his bell, and sent a message to Perks that he should be glad if he would get on with the

Statement of Claim in the Bartleet case, and settled down to give his new client prolonged attention.

"You've got to prosecute," he said at last, "and it seems as though you'll have the right one in the dock. From what you tell me, I should say that nine-tenths of the trouble you've had started from her. And I should say you can feel sure of getting a conviction. But, from what you say, it's not going to be a walkover. She'll get a lot of sympathy from the jury—the more women we can get on it the better—and we shall have to take the line that we're only prosecuting with reluctance, because we couldn't get her to behave any other way.

"There's another thing—we've got to get Bulfit. We've got to get him at once, before the other side makes a move in the same direction."

Mr. Gilson looked serious. "Bulfit," he said, "would be an expensive man."

"So he will. But you'll find it better to win with him than to lose with one of the second string. But we won't rush the fence. I'll tell you what I'll do. I'll write to the young woman, and require a public retraction. She may see the wisdom of giving it, when she's cooled down and taken legal advice. There aren't many of her class who would like the idea of a seat in the Bow Street dock.

"If you get a retraction that you can advertise, you'll have got home by a short cut, and, if you don't, you'll be able to tell the court that you didn't prosecute till you'd done everything else possible, short of taking the law into your own hands.

"And as to Bulfit, I'll just ring his clerk up, and tell him there may be a brief coming along. After that, he'll reckon we've got the first call. You'll find that'll do the trick. He gets twenty-five percent of his business from this address."

Mr. Gilson left the active-minded young lawyer in better spirits than he had come. He felt the relief which is common to those who gain support in conflict, even if it be no more than that for which the purse will pay. And he was impressed by Mr. Plumer's attitude—he had recognized the difficulties of the position, but had maintained a tone of confidence that they would be overcome.

And there was still a chance that the cost and worry of a prosecution would be avoided.

If not, Mr. Gilson reflected vainly, he would have a clear understanding as to what his financial responsibility was to be. He was actually so ignorant of the legal racket that he supposed that it would be possible to get Mr. Bulfit's brief marked with a moderate fee, such as he would be able and willing to pay.

122

CHAPTER XXXIV.

ARABELLA WILL NOT GIVE WAY

"WHYEVER," Muriel asked, when they had reached their own room, "did you say such a dreadful thing?"

"I just thought I would," Arabella replied. "It was Mr. Jellipot's idea, rather than mine."

"I shouldn't have thought—" Reggie began, and was interrupted by: "Of course not. He didn't say it. But he made it quite plain."

Reggie, still unconvinced, saw the wisdom of leaving her with the last word. He said: "Well we've got to move fast now. We might be in a nasty hole if Gilson starts anything before we've got more proof than we have yet."

Arabella approved this remark, both for its plural form, and as justifying the course she had taken. Already it had wakened Reggie up! How right Mr. Jellipot always was!

But that gentleman's mind was not disturbed during the following day by any intimation of the surprising interpretation which Arabella had put upon her last conversation with him. It passed without anything occurring to bring the Briggs murder to his mind, unless the fact that Reggie Tudor asked for time off during the afternoon could be so defined. But next morning the solicitor had a phone call from Miss Arabella Reeves, who wished to see him as soon as he would be disengaged.

"I am always pleased to see you," Mr. Jellipot replied, "but I shall be fully engaged during this afternoon. Perhaps tomorrow or Friday morning would do equally well?"

"I'm afraid it wouldn't. I've had a letter from Mr. Gilson's solicitors, and I want you to reply."

"Perhaps you had better read me the letter."

Arabella did this, and Mr. Jellipot's face, as he listened, showed surprise which gave place to a more serious expression. But he only said: "Yes. I must see you. But it's not easy to fit it in. You'd better go straight to Bentley's. Be there at one o'clock, and wait for me till I can come."

When he had rung off, he cancelled a lunch appointment with Sir Reginald Crowe, who was not pleased, for the matter which would have occupied them was of major financial importance, and gave shorter time to a succession of interviews than they would otherwise have had, by which means he arrived at the table which Arabella had engaged within ten minutes of that young lady's arrival.

Lunch being ordered, he said: "Before you tell me anything, I should like to read that letter again."

Arabella drew it from her bag, and passed it to him. He read:

Dear Madam,

Our client, Mr. Henry Gilson, of the Regent Street Hotel, W.1, has informed us of the gross and groundless accusations against himself which you made both in writing and in the hearing of numerous witnesses in the dining room of that hotel at or about 7:15 P.M. yesterday, the 14th inst.

We understand that you accused him publicly of the murder of your late uncle, Mr. Adrian Briggs, and expressed your intention of repeating this dreadful and baseless slander.

Naturally, our client cannot accept such a position, and we must ask you for an immediate and unqualified apology and withdrawal, together with an undertaking that there will be no repetition of such statements, which apology and undertaking must be published at your expense, in three daily and one weekly periodicals of our client's selection.

On these terms, our client is generously willing to regard the statements made as an exhibition of unbalanced hysteria, but otherwise he must take such a course as the law provides for his protection.

Yours faithfully,

Plumer, Plumer & Plumer

Mr. Jellipot considered this letter for a few seconds in silent disfavour. It lacked his own precision of language, and he thought it to

124

be about twice as long as its matter required. But he recognized that that matter was formidable in itself, and he knew that Plumer & Co. had the second-best criminal practice in London. He said quietly: "You had better tell me what really happened."

"What they say. There's nothing wrong about that."

"But there must have been some provocation. You wouldn't start things like that in a public room."

"It was what you told me to do."

Mr. Jellipot looked his astonishment. "I beg your pardon," he said. "But I must give that statement a most emphatic denial."

"Well, you said they might dish us unless we did."

Mr. Jellipot became silent. At length he said: "I see what you mean. For the moment, we will not discuss that. Will you tell me, with the clarity which you can always command, exactly what occurred?"

When she had told him, he asked: "What do you propose to do now?"

"I shall do anything you advise, except what they say."

"You are determined not to withdraw what you have written?"

"No. It's what I believe to be true."

"That, of course, could be your only moral justification. The legal position is not precisely the same. Do you fully realise the possible consequences of refusing the apology for which they ask?"

"I suppose he'll have to start an action to fight it out."

"A prosecution would be a more exact word."

"You mean he'll prosecute me?"

"Yes. If he has sufficient courage, and confidence in his own case."

"I don't see how he can have that."

"But I think he may. More than that, he may prove to be right. I am bound to advise you of the seriousness of your position, if you are unable to prove what you have said."

"Then the sooner we get to work on it, the better."

"You are resolved not to withdraw?"

"I shouldn't take back what I said. Not unless it were proved to be wrong. Of course, I would then. I wouldn't take it back because I might get put into prison. I can't say I'm afraid. I know you'll be too much for these Plumer people. But if I were, I shouldn't alter for that."

"No," Mr. Jellipot agreed, "I don't think you would. But you must not rely too much upon me. You would like me to answer this letter?"

"If it's worth answering."

"You think that may be doubtful?"

"I'd rather leave that to you."

"I am glad to have that discretion, though I am inclined to think that it will be best to send a reply."

After these words Mr. Jellipot turned the conversation into other channels, and when Arabella left him, it was with a cheerful confidence that she had passed her troubles into stronger hands than her own.

CHAPTER XXXV.

MR. JELLIPOT WRITES A LETTER

WHEN he got back to his office, Mr. Jellipot telephoned Plumer, Plumer & Plumer, and said that he had been instructed by Miss Arabella Reeves, and that they would hear from him during the following day. He then put the matter out of his mind to deal with more immediate exigencies, and it was not until he was enjoying an after-dinner cigar in his own bachelor home that he directed his thoughts to the problem of that reply, if any, which he should give to Mr. Gilson's solicitors.

He considered, in a scrupulous conscience, whether he had occasion to blame himself for a development which he certainly had not anticipated and did not welcome.

He saw that Arabella, by one irrevocable action, had placed herself in the front of the firing line, beyond rescue or retreat.

The path of safety which had been offered to her—that of apology and withdrawal—was, in his judgment, one of an impossible dishonour, unless it should be prompted by genuine conviction of error, in which case it would become of a compulsory quality. It was one which it would have been against his code of self-respect to entertain under any stress of legal assault, and it was finally dismissed by her own emphatic repudiation.

He saw that, widely as the event had swerved from his anticipations, he had been its originating cause. He hesitated as to whether this lack of foresight should be an occasion of self-reproach, or whether, in legal phrase, cause and effect were too remote to be accepted as a logical consequence.

Whether he should blame himself he remained unsure, but, however that might be, he recognized a responsibility which he must not shirk.

The idea that Ames might be a disguised Gilson had originated in his own mind. The questions which he had given to Reggie Tudor had surely been justified by their results. The difficulty lay in the fact that, while different answers might have affirmatively demonstrated that he had been wrong, those which had been obtained went no further than to show that he might have stumbled upon the truth.

If only he could be more sure of that! He saw that, if Gilson were not Ames, it would be a monstrous wrong to lead a jury to a contrary conclusion, even to save an attractive client from the penalty of her own impetuosity. But was that a practical danger? If Gilson were not Ames, it was inconceivable that an exhaustive enquiry could bring any court to a contrary conclusion.

The actual peril—one that was real and great—was that, even though the two had been one, it might be impossible to establish more than a plausible doubt, on which—the issue being so serious—a cautious jury might decline to condemn him.

Had that been the issue of a straightforward murder trial, there might have been little cause for regret. It is surely better that half a dozen guilty men should escape a verdict of condemnation than that an innocent one should suffer conviction. But if the issue should be one of libel—as now seemed to be the inevitable development—there could be no exoneration of one which did not condemn the other.

"We must," he concluded, "put doubts aside, and go forward on the assumption that I was right at my first guess. If we be in error, the truth will defend itself, to our undoing; but if we hesitate we shall be certainly overcome, whether we be right or wrong."

Having decided this fundamental question, he went on to consider how he should reply to the letter which Arabella had received. To ignore it would have some potential advantages, but it would hardly be consistent with the telephone communication he had already made, and was rejected on a more affirmative ground.

There was a possibility, however slight, that Gilson, if he were really a guilty man, might shrink from instituting a prosecution. The demand which he had instructed his solicitors to make might be no more than a bold bluff, or his courage might fail at a later stage. Against any such wavering, a defiant reply would be most likely to prevail, and so, with the first object of saving Arabella from the perils of a hazardous prosecution, he decided to take that tone.

But having done so, he drafted several replies which he did not like. His mind fluctuated between regard for the immediate effect which the letter might have, and that which would result from it being read in court at a later day. He had a further doubt of whether honour or policy might require that he should associate himself with his client's position. In the end, he decided upon a curt and minatory reply, such as might well intimidate an irresolute man, or cause his advisers to think again.

In the morning, he dictated this:—

Messrs. Plumer, Plumer & Plumer,
7, Hart's Buildings,
Lincoln's Inn, W.C.2.

Dear Sirs,

re Gilson (alias Ames)

My client, Miss Arabella Reeves, duly received your letter of the 15th inst.

I am instructed to reply that she expressed her meaning with precision, and has written nothing which she is disposed to alter or to withdraw.

I may add that the opinions which she expressed coincide with my own.

I suggest that you should consider your client's position very seriously before taking further action in the matter.

Yours faithfully,

E. E. Jellipot

Having dictated this, he summoned his managing clerk.

"Newman," he said, "I want you to get in touch at once with Mr. Bulfit's clerk, and tell him that there is a possibility of a prosecution for libel, *Gilson against Reeves*, in which case I am proposing to send him a brief for the defendant. Interest him in the case, if you can. I don't want the other side butting in first."

"I don't see how we can help that, sir," Newman said doubtfully.

"Possibly not. Obviously, we can't brief counsel until we know that a process is issued. But do what you can." Newman having gone on this errand, Mr. Jellipot summoned Reggie Tudor.

"I expect," he said, "that you are already making enquiries, at Miss Arabella's suggestion, as to the address at which Ames must have converted himself into Gilson on the morning of the murder?"

"Yes, sir. I started on that yesterday afternoon."

"And discovered nothing?"

"Nothing yet, sir. But there's plenty of ground left to go over."

"Then take off all the time you require."

Reggie paused at the door.

"You don't think she's in any serious danger?"

"Law is always dangerous. You have been here long enough to know that. Justice is blind, through which infirmity it does many cruel and foolish things. Miss Arabella has certainly risked a considerable term of imprisonment, or a substantial fine. It is our business to see that the matter ends in a different way."

He spoke in a tone which gave Reggie more confidence than he was able himself to feel, as a good general should.

Newman came back later with a tale of little success. Bulfit had already been approached by the other side, but had made no promise to them. He had said that he could not undertake anything until he had seen the brief.

"He mayn't take it, but, after that, he won't take ours, if he sends it back; he gets too much business from Plumers for that."

"Yes," Mr. Jellipot agreed, "I've no doubt he does. Well, we've done all we can in that direction. Newman, has it ever occurred to you that there must be something wrong with a judicial system which recognizes that its decisions may be influenced by the advocacy which those who seek its protection are able to hire?"

Newman said he didn't see how they could alter that.

By the afternoon post, Mr. Harold Plumer, Junior, received Mr. Jellipot's letter, and whistled aloud as he read it. He went into his partner's room (one of the three Plumers had been cremated earlier in the year), and said: "This Gilson business looks like being a lively do. Jellipot's on his hind legs."

Mr. Gilson, hearing the contents of the letter next morning, took it quietly, and without apparent surprise. He said: "It shows I've got to go on. There'll be no peace for me till I've got a legal decision that I'm not Ames."

"No," Mr. Plumer agreed. "I shouldn't say that there will."

He added that they had better proceed by summons. A warrant (even if it should be granted) might create prejudice, and there was no fear that the young woman would run away. He added privately, to his own mind, that it might be the best thing if she would. It had become a case which he did not like. But it would be no worse handled for that. Most of those whom Plumers defended successfully were guilty men, and that Gilson was such was more than he would be prepared to say. Let him come in about the same time tomorrow, and he would be prepared to give any necessary time to the case.

130

CHAPTER XXXVI.

The Obstinacy of Sir Reginald Crowe

"I HAVE no doubt," Sir Reginald said, "that the young lady is all you would have me believe, and perhaps a bit more. I should be sorry to think that she is destined to totter out of jail in a state of senile decay.

"And I am willing to believe that Gilson, or whatever his real name may be, is the star villain of this decade.

"But all the same, you are asking an impossible thing."

"I am not asking you," Mr. Jellipot replied, with that mild persistence which so often prevailed over stubborn obstacles, "to do anything, so far as I am aware, which would be contrary either to the etiquette of your profession, or the requirements of statute law. I ask you only to ascertain, not to disclose. You cannot say that bankers do not exchange such confidential information among themselves."

"Well, if you were only asking that, you might have been a lot plainer. Besides, it's not sense. What use would that be to you?"

"I do not, of course, say that, if there should be such developments as would convince you that you had evidence essential to—I mean which would place the guilt of a barbarous crime on the right head—"

"Look here, Jellipot. I know what you almost said. It was 'interests of justice', that vile phrase that always comes to Combridge's tongue when he's set on doing something particularly nasty. I don't say that it wouldn't be a banker's duty to give information in his possession, if he saw that it would be the only way to prevent a wrongful conviction, but it's a very different thing to go poking into our customers' affairs to see whether there's anything of the sort which we can turn up. And when it comes to asking other banks to join in the game…!

"Besides, the St. James's don't keep their cheques. It's not the London custom, as you know perfectly well. We do, because we're a

131

North of England bank, and we say the cheques are our property. The customer only pays for the stamps. But the St. James's sends them back, and that wouldn't make it any easier."

"Nor, I should think," Mr. Jellipot replied patiently, "would it be much more difficult. You're not going to tell me that there are not other records—"

"No. That would be going a bit too far. Though I don't know what the St. James's system is. It's an old-fashioned bank, and what they do Heaven may know, but I don't.... But I tell you again that you're asking an impossible thing."

"Then I must ask you again later, and I can only hope that you will be able to tell me without delay then."

Sir Reginald laughed. "Good old Jellipot!" he said. "But you won't get round me like that. What I wanted to see you about was the way the executors of the Wills estate are—" But the conversation turned at that point to matters which were interesting enough, but with which we have no present concern.

Mr. Jellipot left the banker's Lombard Street office with no feeling of discouragement, for he had not expected that his request would meet with a good reception. But he was opening a campaign in which he meant that nothing should be left to avoidable chance, and it was within the next hour that he rang up Lady Crowe, and asked when she would be coming into town.

Mr. Jellipot was a favourite with Evelyn, as she with him, and they had past associations such as cannot leave less than an enduring intimacy. She said: "Oh, I don't know. Anything worth coming in for?"

"Not for you. I want you to do something for me."

"Well, of course. What is it?"

"I don't care to explain on the telephone."

"What about lunch tomorrow? Say the Savoy."

"Yes. One-fifteen?"

"That will do for me. You can't give me a hint? We're not off to New York again?"

"No. I'm sorry to say that it's nothing like that. The fact is, Sir Reginald is making a lot of difficulty about something I've asked him to do."

"Then he ought to have more sense. Let me know what you want. I don't suppose Reggie'll be any real trouble. One-fifteen tomorrow." Evelyn laughed, and rang off.

Mr. Jellipot felt that matters went well. With the two (so different) Reginalds working at opposite angles of the same enquiry, anything discoverable should be quickly exposed. But suppose there were nothing there?

CHAPTER XXXVII.

MR. GILSON WRITES A CHEQUE

"THE issue," Mr. Harold said, "is serious, but extremely simple. The libel was of a nature which justifies criminal proceedings, and, in view of the circumstances of the case, and most particularly of the contents of her solicitor's letter, she cannot deny utterance. The sole remaining plea which would be of any legal avail would be justification.

"If that be set up, the onus of proof is theirs, and we can only wait to deal with the evidence which they will submit. If it be no more than that of those warehouse girls, I should say we've got a walkover. But if there's any other card which they might play, you'd better tell me the worst, whatever it's likely to be."

Mr. Gilson said: "Of course I should tell you anything I knew. I'm not an absolute fool. But what could there be? I can let you have my birth certificate, and some school reports, and such evidences as that to prove I've been Henry Gilson all my life. But how a man sets to work to prove he's never been someone else is rather hard to see."

"Well, there are ways. But there might be a good many cases where it couldn't be done. Fortunately, the law doesn't ask us to do that. As I said, the onus of proof is theirs.

"If you're not Ames—and I'm taking your word for that—their chance of proving you are isn't worth a damn. You'll find Bulfit will turn those two young women upside down and inside out till they won't know their heads from their heels."

"You think we'll need Bulfit?"

"Yes. He's dear, but he's the right man. I had a word with him myself yesterday, and I think we can depend upon his taking the brief."

Mr. Gilson gathered courage to ask: "What fee will he be likely to want? You know I'm not a rich man."

Mr. Harold had not omitted to inform himself on that point, and he did not entirely agree. It was one of those offices which valued a reputation for serving its (mostly criminal) clients well; but its idea of reasonable remuneration had no limit below the resources of those who applied for its protection.

Mr. Harold Plumer, Junior, was normally good-humoured, and capable of kindly impulses. Had a poor man engaged his sympathies, he might have given legal help, and said let the bill go hang. But if another came who had saved five or six hundred pounds through the toil of a laborious life, that was the amount which he should be expected to surrender to those who became active in his defence.

He said: "Oh, Bulfit's not unreasonable. You might let me have a cheque for five hundred, and that'll cover everything till I let you know."

His voice was casual, as though he spoke of no more than a trivial sum, for he had a well-practised technique for such occasions.

Sitting prosperous in his padded chair, he seemed by tone and manner to disparage the vulgarity of discussing money at all. What was it but words you wrote on a cheque? There were those, especially women, who would be so hypnotised by his easy manner, and the atmosphere of the opulent room, that they would feel as though he were presenting them with, or at least creating, the sum which he suggested that they should write. Even a Harley Street specialist could have learnt little from him.

But Mr. Gilson was a businessman of his own kind, though his previous experience of legal charges had been of a different order. He said: "I didn't anticipate that the prosecution would be as expensive as that, and, anyway, I like to know what I am making myself liable for. Could you tell me what you would mark Mr. Bulfit's brief? I believe that is the right term to use."

Mr. Harold controlled an uncomplimentary exclamation, and answered suavely: "No, we couldn't do that. We don't know yet what we can fix up. But if the case goes the right way, that ought not to make any difference to you in the end. It's one where, if we get any sort of a win, we ought to see an order for our costs to be paid by the other side."

Mr. Gilson, without the crudity of exact words, had a dim perception of the legal racket by which, even though it be known by his lawyers, and communicated to counsel, that a litigant cannot pay more than a moderate fee, a brief will be marked at a fantastic figure, in the hope that the costs will ultimately be paid by the other side, in which case the loser's pocket and the taxing master will be the only limiting factors—and there is never much to be feared from him!

After a moment of mutual silence, Mr. Harold added, in his most casual voice: "Oh, well, make it two-fifty, and we'll see how we get on." (He had told his senior partner, half an hour earlier, that Gilson ought to be good for two hundred down, if not a bit more. He hadn't been far wrong.)

With no further words, Mr. Gilson wrote the cheque, and Mr. Harold touched his bell, and, with scarcely a glance at the little strip of tinted paper, handed it to the incoming clerk, with a pleasantly-spoken: "Let Mr. Gilson have a receipt for this."

He addressed his client again: "There's one point we've got to decide at the start. The letter we had from Jellipot repeated the libel, not only on his client's behalf, but on his own. There's a question of how far his letter may be considered privileged, and how far, if at all, it may be regarded as a separate libel. It reads as though it had been deliberately intended to be one. The heading alone: 'Alias Ames,' is enough to suggest that, without what follows. The question is, should we proceed against the woman alone, or Jellipot, or both? But I should like to have counsel's opinion first, if you're anxious to bring him in."

"I hadn't thought of that. What do you advise?"

"Well, a woman gets a jury's sympathy more easily than a man, and she's certainly not supposed to be as alive to the law on these matters as a solicitor's bound to be. But it might raise awkward comments if we were to have a go at him and leave her out, and I don't know that it's likely to help us to have two in the dock.

"Besides, Jellipot must have weighed up that possibility, and he's no fool. We should be doing what he's asked for in a loud voice. It's for you to decide, but I'm inclined to say stick to the girl."

"It is a matter," Mr. Gilson replied, "on which I must rely on your judgment."

"Very well, it's the girl it shall be. If you can look in again at three-thirty, and bring the waiter with you, we'll have the information ready for you to swear."

CHAPTER XXXVIII.

A STRATEGY OF DEFENCE

"THE King," Belle said, "seems to be taking a lot of interest in the matter."

Mr. Jellipot glanced at the familiar wording of the summons which she had handed to him, and agreed that it was consistent with that deduction. "Actually," he said, "there are many things done in his name of which he is not separately aware."

"Well," she replied, "I dare say he'll know more about it before it's over." Her voice was as quiet and musical as ever, but it had a faint note of suppressed excitement, which her solicitor did not fail to hear.

"It is," he said, "a new experience for you, and may appear more formidable for that reason. We who are familiar with the persons of which a court is composed when—shall say when the wigs are off?—no, I meant no allusion to Robert Ames, it was a fortuitous parallel—know how little reason there is to be daunted by such as they. Contempt of court may be quite easy to feel. Not that many of them are not honourable and most able men. And the law which they represent is a formidable and sometimes a blundering power."

"I'm not going to crack up, if you mean that."

"I certainly did not intend any such implication. If I should give you any advice—which I am not sure that you need—it would be that, when you are in the witness box, you will not let anything tempt you to speak in haste. If you think first, and say exactly what you mean, the most subtle advocate may be baffled in any pitfall he tries to dig."

"I've no doubt you are right, and it's advice that I won't forget. But it seems to me that everything must depend upon what proofs we can get together. If we can't prove he's Ames, nothing I say, or don't, is likely to be much good to me; and if we prove that, nothing else is likely to be much harm to us, or much good to him."

"It is acutely said. And I wish I could reply that I am satisfied with the proofs we have. I can say no more than that I am sure that, unless we are wrong—which we must not now allow ourselves to debate—such proofs must exist, and that I have thought of a way by which one of them should be brought to light, even though Mr. Tudor's commendably persistent efforts should have no direct result."

"I knew you'd think of something." Belle's voice, as she said this, had a note of gratitude which Mr. Jellipot felt to be premature, and which he would have been relieved to feel was no more out of place than that. He changed the subject to ask: "When did you have this document—yesterday afternoon, or this morning?"

"I had it yesterday. There was a man waiting with it when we got back from the matinee at the Haymarket."

"I see." In fact, he saw more than he intended to say. It was almost conclusive that no similar process had been issued against himself, about which he was less than pleased, but which it was essential to know before he could make final decisions concerning the strategy of the defence. Nor did she enquire as to what he meant, for his question had brought another matter before her mind.

"They've turned Mr. Gilson out of the hotel."

"How did you learn that?"

"Alice told us—the chambermaid. There's no doubt they've done it."

"It seems rather like prejudging the issue."

"Oh, it isn't exactly that. But they don't like rows at the hotel, and I suppose they thought while we were both there.... And then we've got our rooms for three months, and Mr. Gilson's been there by the week."

"Yes. There would be reason in that. And perhaps now that he has finished with Kilburn, he hasn't the same cause for keeping a hotel room."

Mr. Jellipot's mind, trained to separate probability from report, actually imagined very nearly what had occurred: a discreet suggestion by the management, which was yet legally less than a request to leave, and Gilson's carelessly worded reply (which may have been true) that he had been already decided to leave at the week's end. It had been no more than that, but it was evidence (had any been needed) of the deadly nature of the conflict on which they had entered, in which there could now be no mercy, and from which there could be no retreat.

Fundamentally, the position was that she had arrogated to herself what the community claimed as its collective right. She had pronounced a verdict of guilty against Henry Gilson, and, unless that verdict should be approved by her fellow countrymen, it was a fault which their laws could not condone.

Mr. Jellipot dismissed from his mind a matter in which they had no direct concern. "There are two points," he said, "on which I ought to take your instructions, though I should say that they raise little doubt in my own mind, which has reached conclusions with which I feel sure that you will concur.

"The first question relates to the two young women whose statements are so largely responsible for the present position. Should we seek their friendly co-operation, and invite them to attend as our willing witnesses, or should we avoid any further contacts, and subpoena them to attend the court?"

"We've got till next Tuesday. There's plenty of time for me to see them, if that's what you'd like me to do."

"But I shouldn't like it at all. The further that you—and Tudor also—keep away from them, the better I shall be pleased. In any case, they are bad witnesses. What they told you may have been true. I have little doubt that it was. But I suppose that they would both lie at very short notice, and almost no provocation. It might be fatal for it to appear that they are being prompted by us. Fortunately, there are the statements they made to the police, which, under appropriate circumstances, we might be able to put in. We may also have grounds for asking the court to treat them as hostile witnesses."

"I don't see why they should be that."

"Nor do I. Beyond the fact that the statements they made were, if I was correctly informed, accompanied by some assurance that they would not be required to repeat them in public. It was one which, had it been possible to foresee this development, it would have been improper to give."

"You'll say that's my fault again."

"Scarcely that. We may well wait till a later day before attempting to apportion merit or blame. But it is certain that a prosecution for libel was a contingency which I, at least, did not forecast. The other point which must be settled is the selection of counsel for the defence."

"I thought you'd do that yourself."

"Which might be a great mistake. It is true that you are entitled to be represented by your solicitor before the magistrate, but, as I think you understand already, that will only be a preliminary hearing. It may be conclusive—that is, the charge against you may be dismissed. But if there should be a committal—if it should be sent to a higher court—I could not represent you there.

"But my particular reason for proposing that we should have counsel in the magistrate's court is that I propose to give evidence there, and though that is no legal bar to my appearing as your advocate, there are practical considerations."

"Of course, if you think it best."

"So I do. And there are one or two counsel—in particular, Thirsk—who specialise on the law of libel, and among whom it may seem natural to choose."

"But I must advise you differently. On the issue of libel, there is no occasion for particular knowledge, for there can be no obscure points of law which it could be useful to raise. Had they proceeded against me also, the position would have been somewhat different, but they have been too wily for that.

"Our defence is that the words you wrote were true, which would not in itself be a complete legal answer. But we can add that it was in the public interest that they were uttered, which would be undeniable, for it is not in the public interest that a murderer should remain at large.

"The sole question is: can we establish that which we assert? And that is where a man like Luton, or Berwick Law, someone more accustomed to practise in the criminal courts, someone who can stand up to Bulfit—may be preferable."

"Everyone seems afraid of Bulfit."

"He is a good advocate, and particularly skilful in cross-examination."

"Well, he can't make black white."

"There have been counsel who have won as many as seventy percent of their cases, which suggests that they sometimes do."

"You mean the judges aren't quite as clever?"

"That may have occasional truth. But it is in the swaying of juries that such men excel. Fortunately, we shall be before Rentoul."

"You mean Sir Charles Rentoul?"

"Yes. You know him?"

"I met him once. He's a dear. But I shouldn't think he'd be much good in a legal battle."

"That will not be precisely his part. But he has the reputation of being the strongest magistrate in the Metropolitan area. He is one, at least, whom Mr. Bulfit's methods will not intimidate. There is a well-remembered incident when he rebuked the Attorney-General as casually as though he had been a young solicitor fumbling through his first case."

Belle looked puzzled. She had a clear memory of a very courteous elderly gentleman, with kindly-smiling eyes, and most gentle manners. Could it be the same? Yes, there could be no doubt about that.

"I shan't mind much," she said, "if it's only he."

"You will make an error," Mr. Jellipot said, "if you think you will have favours from him. He will see that you have exact justice, and that Gilson has it no less. He will not allow himself to be overborne either by Bulfit or your own advocate. You must expect nothing beyond that."

"Well, that's all we ought to," she agreed indifferently, but her heart was lighter than it had been, in its illogical feminine way. Sir Charles Rentoul? There couldn't be much to be feared from *him*.

CHAPTER XXXIX.

Mr. Bulfit Opens the Case

SIR REGINALD CROWE, with Evelyn at his side, was in the crowded corridor of the court. They were surrounded by bad-tempered people who, like themselves, were confronted by a closed door, and their own tempers—or, at least, Sir Reginald's, were not good.

"I told you, Evelyn," he said, "that you were only wasting my time.

"Well," his wife replied, with cheerful logic, "you're not going to waste as much as though we had got in. You can be in Lombard Street in about ten minutes, and we can try again when they get hungry and go to lunch."

"You can, if you like. But you won't get me here again."

"Reggie, don't be a pig."

It will never be known what response the indignant chairman of the London & Northern Bank would have made to this admonition, for a voice at his elbow interposed: "If you'll please come this way, Sir Reginald," and next moment Mr. Jellipot's managing clerk was leading them to a further door.

Sir Reginald looked at Newman with puzzled eyes. "How did Mr. Jellipot know we were coming?"

"Mr. Jellipot usually provides for eventualities, sir."

Sir Reginald turned with dawning apprehension to meet Evelyn's too-innocent glance. "Good old Jellipot!" he said, with a short laugh. "So you're both in it? And the sob stuff's to get me down? If that's the game, I'll say you deserve more than you're likely to get."

"Of course, I knew you'd see through it at once," Evelyn said placidly. But now, with a sign for silence, Newman was leading them through another door, and looking back to say: "It's all right. Sir Charles isn't in yet." And so, by a way not meant for them, they joined the little group in the front of the crowded court, from which Mr. Jellipot turned with a word of greeting.

"It was good of you to come," he said quietly.

"Miss Reeves needs all the support she's likely to get. Let me introduce you."

He touched Belle's arm, and she broke off a conversation with Mr. Berwick Law to shake hands with the banker and his attractive wife.

She did not feel very frightened, now that the ordeal was upon her. It had seemed far worse as she had turned over, vainly seeking sleep, during the night. The court was smaller than she had expected. And everything seemed rather informal in the rustling whispering prelude before the magistrate had appeared. And she was surrounded by numerous friends, Reggie Tudor among them, the results of whose persistent canvassing of the neighbourhood of Antrobus Road were not yet certain, even to Mr. Jellipot, and certainly not to him.

Muriel also was there, giving an inscrutably confident support to the impetuosity of her younger sister, as the hour approached at which the law would determine whether Belle really shouldn't have said that.

And Inspector Combridge had spoken an encouraging word a few moments earlier, making her feel that the police were not without friendly willingness to give her what aid they could.

She had had a conference at his chambers with Berwick Law, and his almost offhand presumption that it was Gilson's hand which had drawn the razor across his partner's throat had been very comforting, though she had wit enough to see that it might be no more than the attitude which he thought would be best for her. No less, it did something to reduce a doubt which had been persistent to vex her mind since it had become too late for any doubt to avail.

Mr. Bulfit had just given her one swift appraising glance, which shifted instantly as it met her own, and even he did not look nearly as dreadful as she had been led to fear.

"I was telling Miss Reeves," Berwick Law said, "that when she hears the case called, she should be ready for the usher to guide her into the dock. It is one in which most magistrates would allow her a seat in front of it, but that is a point on which Sir Charles will never make any exceptions."

"I don't see that that matters. I suppose I can sit down?"

"Oh, yes. Only wait till Sir Charles gives you permission."

Belle laughed. "Oh, well! If the law likes being rude—" At which words her counsel looked at her critically. Should a warning be given? Perhaps it would do more harm than good. When he had talked to her yesterday, she had seemed an exceptionally sensible girl. And good-looking—which, if this case should go to trial, on which the odds were ten to one, if not more, might be more important still. But now there was the stir of rising, as Sir Charles Rentoul entered, bowed to the court, seated himself, and looked round with a glance which seemed to observe nothing in particular, and actually took in everything which it was his business to know, the while the crowded benches settled again for the drama which was to come.

The next moment, the magistrate's clerk, sitting below him, was calling the case. Mr. Bulfit, half rising, said that he was for the prosecutor. Mr. Berwick Law, with a similarly perfunctory motion, said that he was for the defendant. Yes, she was present. The next moment she was in the dock, to be released no more till the case should be finally concluded, unless with the consent of the law she had so rashly challenged. She looked up from her lower place at a magistrate whose eyes rested upon her without sign of recognition. She was permitted to take a seat.

There was a moment's pause while Mr. Bulfit turned over the pages of his brief and consulted Mr. Plumer upon a marginal note, on which the solicitor whispered to Mr. Gilson, sitting at his side, before replying; and then Mr. Bulfit rose, and commenced to state his client's case with the lucid brevity for which he had a well-established repute.

"The circumstances," he said, "are of such a nature as have left the prosecutor no possible course but to seek the protection of the law against an allegation which, had there been no more than casual slander, he might have felt able to ignore, in view of its inherent absurdity, which, it might be argued with reason, should render it incredible to any well-balanced mind.

"These circumstances, which I shall call my client to prove, but most of which are common ground, and beyond serious challenge, are briefly these:

"Mr. Henry Gilson comes before the court as a man of good character, a Londoner, born in Balham, and having resided continuously in the neighbourhood of this metropolis. He will produce his birth certificate, his school records, photographs at different ages, and other abundant evidences to sustain his continuous identity, until, some years ago, he established himself in the Strand as a dealer in stamps.

"Having traded successfully in what, I believe, is often a very lucrative business, he found himself, less than a year ago, with a substantial sum in hand, for which he required investment.

"With that object in view, he answered an advertisement in the *Morning Post*, and received an answer from the office of Mr. E. E. Jellipot, a well-known city solicitor, stating that the business in question was that of Briggs & Co., Kilburn, and giving some preliminary particulars.

"Following this, he had interviews with Mr. Jellipot, with a Mr. Robert Ames, the manager of the firm, and with the proprietor, Mr. Adrian Briggs. It appeared that the business was short of capital, but otherwise sound, and after such further investigations as a prudent businessman would naturally make, he became a partner—a more or less sleeping partner—with Adrian Briggs, investing a substantial amount of capital, and agreeing that Ames should retain the management of the business under some increased supervision.

"So far, there is nothing to observe but an ordinary commercial transaction, and, so far as the prosecutor is concerned, I may say that there never has been anything with which he has been even remotely connected which cannot be so described.

"But when this partnership had endured for no more than a few weeks, there came a day when Adrian Briggs, who was a late riser, was found at midday by his housekeeper murdered in his bed. That it was murder was a fact of which, I think, there can be little doubt, the circumstances being such as to render it almost impossible that he should have died by his own hand, or in any accidental manner.

"I am instructed that Robert Ames admitted that he had been with the dead man between 9:30 and 10:30, or thereabouts, that morning, and that there was no evidence that anyone else had been near the room in which the crime had been committed. As to the guilt or innocence of Robert Ames, it does not appear to me to be the duty of this prosecution, nor might it be proper, to make any suggestion. It is a fact that he was invited by Chief Inspector Combridge, who is present in court, and can be called if necessary, to accompany him to Scotland Yard, and that he thereupon disappeared, and has not been found.

"It was a natural result of his own conduct that he put himself under grave suspicion, but with that we have nothing to do.

"It has been established, I believe to the satisfaction of the police, that, though my client—as he was the first to tell them—was in the vicinity of Antrobus Road on the morning of the murder, he did not enter the house. It might be thought that, in such circumstances, not even the wildest hypothesis could attribute the crime to him, and that no fair-minded person would make such an attempt.

"But Mr. Gilson will tell the court that almost immediately after the discovery of the crime, Robert Ames telephoned him to say that

145

he—Henry Gilson—had been seen near Antrobus Road at about the time the murder occurred, and to make the gratuitous and offensive offer that he would keep silent upon the fact.

"Mr. Gilson's instant reply was that which would be natural to any honest and innocent man—he told Ames that his silence was not required, and he promptly informed the police, without reservation, of his movements upon the morning in question, and of the business reasons which caused them. They were such as to convince the police as, I am sure, Chief Inspector Combridge would tell the court, that he could not, by any possibility, be associated with the crime."

Mr. Bulfit paused to flick over two pages of his brief, to which he had so far made little reference as he pursued the smooth course of his narrative, and the magistrate, who had been glancing at the sworn information before him, as though seeking elucidation of what he heard, said: "One moment, Mr. Bulfit. I should like to be quite clear. The libel of which your client complains is based upon the allegation that he is not Gilson, but Ames. You say that he has convincing proofs of his identity, and, if that be so—I am not, of course, prejudging the issue in any way—it seems evident that the defence could not be sustained. But I fail to see how the innocence of Gilson can be at issue, the libel not asserting that Gilson committed the murder, but that it was the act of Ames, and that your client is he.

"If this be so, it appears to involve the surprising theory that the admittedly innocent Gilson has fled instead of the suspected Ames, and that the suspected Ames remains in the name of Gilson. It is a proposition which I will not discuss at this stage, beyond saying that it is a matter about which it does not seem possible that there could be an enduring doubt after proper enquiry had been made. But, as I understand the information which your client has sworn, the question of the innocence of Gilson does not arise. Let him prove that he is Gilson, and he will have proved all that his case requires."

Bulfit was quick to see the very natural error into which the magistrate had fallen, but he paused for one brief moment, as he considered how he could use it most effectually to ridicule the defendant's case in his reply; and in that instant Berwick Law saved him the trouble, by rising, and saying briefly: "We say that Ames was guilty, but we do not therefore say that Gilson is innocent. Quite the contrary. We say that Ames and Gilson are the same man."

Sir Charles began: "But surely, if that were so—" and checked himself abruptly. His face became blank of expression as he said: "Pray go on, Mr. Bulfit."

From that moment, he listened closely, but said nothing further, and gave no indication of what he thought.

CHAPTER XL.

MR. BULFIT CONTINUES

MR. BULFIT glanced down at his brief again, and turned a further sheet with an impatient hand. It dealt with the departure of Clara Shole, and he saw that it was of no advantage to him. When the other side put her into the box—as they would be obliged to do—he would know how to deal with *her*. But she was of no affirmative advantage to him.

He went on: "The next incident to which it is necessary to call attention, and the one in which the defendant is first heard of as endeavouring to connect Henry Gilson with the death of Adrian Briggs (I should have mentioned that she is a niece of the murdered man), concerns the conduct of a warehouse girl, Bessie Butcher, employed by Briggs & Co., who asked Mr. Gilson for an advance in wages, which he refused.

"She came to him again on the next day, with a tale that she had been approached by the defendant, who had been accompanied by one of Mr. Jellipot's clerks, and that they had offered her money to answer some questions concerning Ames. She stated that she had refused to say what they required, and had declined to accept the money, and she then repeated the demand for an increased wage, in a manner which implied that she had placed Mr. Gilson under an obligation by her silence.

"His answer, which I think most of us would approve, was to dismiss her at once.

"But by this time he had become so sensitive to an atmosphere of surrounding suspicion, if not of open hostility, among the workpeople who, by the death of Adrian Briggs, and the flight of Ames, had come under his control, that he had resolved to dispose of his interest in the business, and return to his previous occupation at his Strand office, which he still continued.

"So it might have ended, had he not, during the brief period which elapsed before he severed his connection with it, found himself to be surrounded by an atmosphere of such increasing hostility as he felt to be beyond toleration, and caused him to insert an advertisement—not worded, perhaps, quite as it would have come from a legal pen, offering a reward for a conviction for slander, which is not a criminal offence—but which may be said to have been fully justified by its result.

"On the evening following its insertion, as the prosecutor was dining in public, in the main dining room of the Regent Street Hotel, he was approached by the defendant, who said in such a tone that it must have been clearly heard by many of the surrounding guests, words to this effect: 'I've seen your advertisement, and I say you're Robert Ames, and you murdered my uncle. I can't say it plainer than that.' To aggravate the offence, and, it might seem, with the explicit purpose of challenging this prosecution, she forthwith laid a paper beside Mr. Gilson, which I have here, and which reads: 'I say that you, Henry Gilson, were Robert Ames, and that you killed my uncle. Arabella Reeves.'

"She then walked away, with a remark to the effect that he could take it lying down if he liked.

"Naturally, he did not take it lying down. He remembered what Miss Butcher had said about being approached by the defendant with an offer of money if she would say something which, whatever it may have been, was evidently construed by that young woman as intended to be an attack upon himself; and he concluded that his advertisement had successfully indicated the source of the annoyances to which he had been subjected.

"He considered also that the defendant was a niece of the murdered man, and that indignation at the crime might have done something to upset the balance of an otherwise normal mind. He therefore instructed his solicitors to write her such a letter as would provide an opportunity for withdrawal, and such public apology as should put a final end to the campaign of slander on which she had been engaged.

"As this offer received such a reply from her solicitor as tended to aggravate the offence, he applied forthwith for the summons that has brought us here. I call Mr. Henry Gilson."

Mr. Bulfit's statement contained little with which the readers of this narrative are not already familiar, but, to most of those who heard, it had the novelty which gave edge to its surprising substance. Nor was the gravity of its issue less clearly seen. What could it be but a verdict which would amount to murder against the prosecutor, or the conviction of the defendant of a baseless criminal libel of the most terrible kind, and most audaciously and persistently made?

Mr. Gilson entered the witness box under the intent scrutiny of many curious eyes. Would he vindicate his identity and innocence with triumphant ease, leading to a committal, and ultimate punishment of a defendant who sat passively self-possessed, as though, even now, impervious to the peril which might forfeit her liberty for long years to come? Or would he break down in some dramatic way, which would vindicate her attack, and send him to the hangman's hands?

Either way, the reporters could see that there must be such an end as would give them superlative opportunity of using their queer continual word "sensational"—in next Sunday's papers. Or was the whole case to come to a premature collapse, under the direction of a magistrate who would often intervene with a humanity equal to his knowledge of law, to compose disputes before they led to more misery than the occasion required?

For though Mr. Gilson was in the box, Mr. Bulfit delayed to commence his examination, seeing that Sir Charles was leaning over to discuss something with his clerk, which that gentleman had risen to hear.

The reporters, alert, but listening vainly, could catch no more than "but the police would surely...."—and—"In any case, at this stage"—and then the clerk had resumed his scat, and the magistrate had sat back, and was saying: "Yes, Mr. Bulfit, we will hear what Mr. Gilson has to say."

CHAPTER XLI.

MR. GILSON WAS A GOOD BOY

IT could not be denied that Mr. Gilson was a good witness. He spoke quietly and distinctly; and his replies were definite, and went no further than the questions led.

His counsel conducted him from his birth, through his early years, through the creditable records of two positions he had held before he had started his own business, and up to the time when he answered the Briggs advertisement, and throughout, it was the record of a blameless life.

There appeared to be no doubt that he was Henry Gilson, and that he had been so continuously since he had been photographed in a baby's chair.

Counsel led him on through the partnership negotiations, covering ground already familiar, which need not be trodden again, up to the day of the murder, and the alibi of his interview with Blake on that day.

On subsequent matters, he was brief, which may have been adroit advocacy, passing lightly over what (if any were) might be dangerous ground, but it was a defensible attitude, for the allegation was that he had committed the murder in the person of Robert Ames, and the libel may be said to have ended at that day.

In any case, the allegations were for the defence to prove, there was no necessity for them to be disproved by him.

Mr. Bulfit put his final questions: "You are Henry Gilson, not Robert Ames?"

The witness smiled slightly as he replied: "No. Certainly not."

"And you had no part in the murder of Adrian Briggs?"

"Emphatically not. I think it was an atrocious crime."

Mr. Bulfit sat down, with the consciousness, to which a good advocate is always sensitive, that the court was with him. It may be doubted whether there were a dozen people on its crowded benches

151

who would not have staked any reasonable sum on Belle Reeves ending as a convicted woman.

The usual time for the luncheon interval was already past, and the court's adjournment at this point was an expected thing. Sir Charles had delayed it deliberately to allow of the completion of the examination in chief, and now, as the court rose, he leaned over to the clerk again, and said: "You might let Mr. Bulfit know the view that I take."

Mr. Thaxton nodded, and within the next minute the two legal gentlemen were in a whispered colloquy which the reporter of the *Evening Herald*, apparently busy upon putting his notes in order, strove to follow with exceptional ears.

He heard clearly: "Now that he has vindicated his character...a full apology, and, of course, a full indemnity for all costs incurred. It would be a magnanimous thing."

He thought that the attitude of the prosecuting counsel was not antagonistic. Perhaps the case was destined, after all, to an early collapse. He might even be back at the office in time to go out with Miss Tonks for tea.

He did not observe Mr. Jellipot hand some folded foolscap sheets to Sir Reginald Crowe, who did not receive them readily, nor hear the solicitor's words: "Yes, you made that quite plain. But, all the same, they'd save you a lot of time, if you should decide differently."

CHAPTER XLII.

Mr. Jellipot Will Go On

IT was within five minutes of the time when the court would resume its sitting that Mr. Plumer's search for Mr. Jellipot ended in
the solicitors' room.

"I've heard," he said, "and I should think it's good news for
you, that Rentoul's willing to let your client down with as little
bump as he can, if we'll stand for that. And I've told Gilson he's got
all he needs, if we call it a day now.

"He's never been after money. He'd have brought a civil action
for that. And if he gets a proper apology now—"

"Yes," Mr. Jellipot replied, "I can see that. My difficulty is that
the vindication of your client's character is not the object at which I
am instructed to aim."

"You mean it's going to be a bit of a climb down for you? Well,
I don't even see that. You'll find that most people will say she's
been well advised, and that you've got her very cleverly out of the
mess."

"So I must hope that they will," Mr. Jellipot replied placidly.
"Shall we go in now?"

Mr. Plumer, though not a slow-witted man, was puzzled by the
implications of this reply.

"Naturally," he said, "we shall expect— Anyway, I should say
it's the last chance you're likely to get."

"You may naturally," Mr. Jellipot retorted, "be considering the
interests of your client, rather than mine."

They went in with no further words.

Mr. Jellipot, glancing round the reassembling court, observed,
with a qualified satisfaction, that Newman was guiding Lady Crowe
to her seat, but that Sir Reginald had not returned. His eyes fell also
on the two warehouse girls whom he had subpoenaed, sitting together on a side bench. Clara, who had perceptibly degenerated

since she had exchanged the packing of micrometers for the serving of half pints in the Turks' Head bar, was looking sullenly in his direction. Bessie was engaged in apparently amicable conversation with a uniformed constable near the door.

Mr. Jellipot made a difficult way toward Lady Crowe. "Sir Reginald," he asked, "was not able to get back?"

"I don't know what he's doing," Evelyn replied, smiling at a recollection she did not intend to recount fully. "We didn't have lunch together. He was in the worst temper I ever knew. He said you seemed to have got your client into the soup this time, and you don't care much who you pull in, as long as you get her out."

"I wish I could know in the next minute what the result of his enquiries will be," Mr. Jellipot replied, with apparent inconsequence, which Evelyn had no difficulty in understanding.

"Not," he told himself, with characteristic mental honesty, "that a negative result would incline me to accept the offer which has been made; but it would certainly lead me to consult my client thereon, which I do not now propose to do, preferring to follow the instructions I already have."

As he thought this, he saw that Mr. Thaxton was looking in his direction, with evident intention of effecting a nearer contact. Next moment he had reached his side, and was saying: "Sir Charles asked me to ascertain whether you expect to finish this afternoon, or shall you want a second day?"

It was a natural and proper enquiry to make. The business of the court could not be conducted with economy of time if such matters were not intelligently forecast. The legal representatives of an accused person are alone able to say how long their cross-examinations are likely to last, or how many witnesses they propose to call. But they both understood that the question which had really been asked was of another kind. If an avenue of settlement could be opened by the magistrate, would Mr. Jellipot advise his client to assent to a course which, even at this late hour, would save her from the worst consequences of that reckless libel?

Mr. Jellipot responded with equal obliquity, but his reply was unmistakable in its implication: "I should estimate that the cross-examination of Gilson will occupy an hour, if not more. I believe that the prosecution have one other witness, whose testimony will be brief, and whom we are not likely to challenge. They may like to call Combridge also, but I think they will be more likely to leave him to us. But the evidence of our own witnesses is a different matter. We are not likely to occupy less than a second day."

The magistrate's clerk accepted this with an expressionless face. He said: "Then you will require an adjournment. Would this day week be convenient?"

"It would be convenient both to Berwick Law and myself," Mr. Jellipot answered. (The convenience either of the prosecutor or the defendant is not considered in these skirmishes.) "But, if there should be such an interval, I hope that there will be no difficulty about recognisances?"

"They are likely to be substantial."

"There would be no difficulty about that. Lady Crowe has kindly promised—and Sir Phillip Reeves will be here before the court is due to rise. And I myself am prepared to undertake any required sum."

Mr. Thaxton said that, in that case, he was sure that no difficulty would arise. But Sir Charles might prefer to sit again tomorrow, and go straight on.

Mr. Jellipot, having thus assured himself that a week's adjournment would not result in a period of incarceration for his client (magistrates are sometimes more difficult about granting bail during the course of such an enquiry than upon its completion) replied that either course would be convenient to him. But, by this time, the magistrate had returned to court, and Mr. Gilson to the witness box, and Mr. Jellipot must squeeze into his own seat behind Mr. Berwick Law, who had risen to commence his cross-examination.

CHAPTER XLIII.

Mr. Gilson Is Cross-Examined

MR. BERWICK LAW began: "Now, Mr. Gilson, will you tell the court what hours you usually gave to your business in the Strand?"

"There were no fixed hours."

"Shall we say two hours daily?"

"It was much more than that."

"Three?"

"I have said that there were no fixed hours."

"The office is usually closed?"

"It is usually open during the day."

"Usually in the afternoons rather than in the mornings?"

"I should not say that. I sometimes arrive late."

"You would not deny it?"

"I have said that I have no regular hours. It is mainly a correspondence business."

"No doubt it is. What staff do you employ?"

"None. It does not require it."

"No regular hours, and no staff. You have told the court that you reside in a flat at Streatham. You are a single man?"

"Yes."

"Perhaps you keep a resident housekeeper?"

"No. I employ a daily woman who gives all the service that I require."

"So that no one would know however short or irregular your visits to your flat may be?"

"Do you really think that to be a logical deduction from what I have said?"

"You must please answer the question. You must not question me."

Mr. Bulfit was on his feet: "I submit that the question invited the retort which it received. It was not a reasonable deduction from what the witness had said. It was, indeed, of the nature of argument rather than fact."

Sir Charles Rentoul smiled upon the contending barristers. "Perhaps, Mr. Berwick Law, you could frame your question rather differently."

"I will put it this way. Can you, Mr. Gilson, give the name of any person who would know if you only slept in that flat two nights a week?"

"I have never considered the matter. I suppose there would be several."

"Such as?"

"There would be the caretakers and neighbours."

"On which floor is the flat?"

"On the top floor."

"And on which do the caretakers live?"

"In the basement."

"And how much would they know of what goes on at the top floor?"

"I have no idea. But I should like to say that I was often absent for several days at a time prior to my connection with Briggs & Co., and after that I only used the flat for weekends, as I found it more convenient to reside at the Regent Street Hotel. When I had nothing except the stamp business to keep me in London, I was often away. I stayed frequently, for instance, at Southview House, Brighton, as I have no doubt that their books would show."

"You are aware that Robert Ames was also a single man, and also lived in the same solitary way?"

"No, I know nothing about it."

"You had business relations with Mr. Ames of a rather intimate character, and were really unaware of those circumstances?"

"They were strictly business relations. He was not a man with whom I should have chosen to have any other personal contacts."

"And you were really unaware that he was a single man?"

"I was not interested. In any case I am here to say what I know, and not hearsay reports."

"That's one for you, Berwick," Mr. Bulfit said, in an undertone that reached the reporters' table.

Mr. Berwick Law was stooping backwards to take a whispered word from Mr. Jellipot. He turned to address the magistrate: "It might be a convenient method, and save the time of the court, if the cross-examination of Mr. Gilson should be deferred at this stage until some witnesses for the defence have been heard."

Mr. Bulfit was rising, apparently to protest, as Sir Charles Rentoul turned his eyes in his direction: "It is not a request which I can refuse, Mr. Bulfit, in such a matter as this, but you will, of course, have an opportunity of re-examining. The signing of the prosecutor's deposition will be deferred till it is complete."

The examination of witnesses in such an enquiry is always a slow process, owing to the necessity of recording both questions and answers in writing for the signatures of these concerned, and for subsequent use when the case is tried in the higher court. The afternoon was now advanced, and it would have appeared most improbable, a minute before, that the case for the defence would be opened before the next hearing.

But, being asked if he had more witnesses, Mr. Bulfit replied: "I have a waiter here from the Regent Street Hotel, but his evidence is not required, if the account of the scene there, as given by the prosecutor, is not in dispute."

Mr. Berwick Law said he was prepared to accept it as substantially accurate.

Asked if he had anything more to say, Mr. Bulfit replied that, as the cross-examination of the prosecutor was not completed, he might have to ask for an opportunity to address the court at a later stage; but, so far as he could see at present, the defence consisted in requiring the prosecutor to prove that he was not Robert Ames, which he was under no obligation to do.

Mr. Law showed no disposition to challenge this attitude. The rights of addressing the court at various stages are conditional upon points of procedure which may be the subject of much manoeuvring for position when a jury is in the box, but it was of minor importance now, especially as a committal was regarded as a certainty by the legal gentlemen on both sides, unless there should be such a collapse of the prosecutor's case as would make forensic eloquence of no avail before a magistrate of Sir Charles Rentoul's independence of judgment.

Now Sir Charles addressed the defendant directly, stating with legal precision the charge which had been made against her, and directing her that she was under no obligation to make reply, or to call witnesses, but that she was free to do so, in which case anything which might be said would become evidence which might be used if she should be put on trial before a higher court.

Belle listened to this admonition with the attention natural to one so nearly concerned, but with no acuter emotion, for she had been told what to expect, and knew that Mr. Berwick Law would undertake the answer on her behalf. Beyond that, though she had as yet no tendency to go to sleep in the dock (which has been known to occur), she was conscious of the curious feeling of detachment produced by the method of English judicial proceeding, which puts the one most concerned on one side, as no more than an exhibit in the case, or the spectator of a conflict he does not share.

This position is less absolute than was the case before an accused person was allowed to give evidence on his own behalf, but, even so, except when actually in the witness box, it is the price of engaging legal assistance that he shall remain silent, and he is the one person concerned in the case whose attention may wander at will without detriment or remark.

"Our reply," Mr. Berwick Law was saying, "is simply that the words of which the prosecutor complains are true, and that it is in the public interest that their truth should be disclosed, which could have been secured in no other way. The defendant will give her own evidence to this effect. I call Miss Arabella Reeves."

The door of the dock opened, and the usher guided her to the witness box.

CHAPTER XLIV.

Belle in the Box

MR. BERWICK LAW guided his client through the preliminary stages of her testimony with a practised agility which even Mr. Bulfit could not excel; and, like Mr. Bulfit, he was assisted by the clearness and cogency of the replies which he received.

Sir Charles Rentoul, inscrutably watchful of a drama the end of which he owned to himself that he was unable to guess, was increasingly puzzled by what he heard.

He had supposed that the witness box would reveal the character of the young woman who had sat with such restrained quietude in the dock as hysterical, spiteful, or of a mental balance abnormally disturbed by the tragedy of her uncle's death.

But her replies were clearly given, without hesitation, ambiguity, or discursiveness, as she told of her conviction that Robert Ames had been her uncle's murderer (about which there might be general agreement), and of her determination, when it had appeared that the police were unable to find him, that the enquiry should not be dropped.

She went on to tell a breathless court how she had sought Mr. Jellipot's assistance, and of the three questions which he had given to Reggie Tudor, who had shown them to her, and of her two talks with Bessie Butcher, with the replies which they had received.

"And what effect had these statements on your mind?" her counsel asked.

"They convinced me that Robert Ames and Henry Gilson are the same man "

"Had you any other reason for arriving at this conclusion?"

"There was what I heard that Clara Shole had said, and why she had left."

"What was that?"

Mr. Bulfit was on his feet at once: "I protest against both that question and the previous one, and the reply which was given. Whatever hearsay gossip the witness may have heard cannot be evidence which the court can consider."

"I submit," Berwick Law replied, "that the witness is entitled to tell the court of all the influences which led her to the conclusions to which she came. She is entitled to disclose anything which tends to show that she did not proceed through malice, or without reasonable cause."

Sir Charles Rentoul asked: "Are you calling Miss Shole, Mr. Berwick Law?"

"I have subpoenaed her, and she is now present in court."

"Then it will be best to have her own testimony. But I must rule that the defendant is entitled to say that she was influenced by statements made by Miss Shole, but it may be best to leave unsaid what those statements were. You will not object to that, Mr. Law?"

Mr. Law said he was content, and Mr. Bulfit, who was less so, but knew that it was useless to ask for more than he was going to get, subsided on to his seat.

The examination continued: "And was that all?"

"No. There was something Mr. Jellipot told me which seemed conclusive.

Sir Charles spoke quickly, before there was time for further protest, or for the recording of the reply: "You are calling Mr. Jellipot?"

"He will be my next witness."

"Very well. We will have his own testimony of whatever he may have told the defendant. Pray go on, Mr. Law."

"From this aggregate of evidence, what opinion did you finally form?"

"I became convinced that Robert Ames and Henry Gilson are the same man, and that he murdered my uncle."

"Are you still of that belief?"

"Yes, I have no doubt at all."

Mr. Berwick Law said that that completed his examination, and Sir Charles said that it would be convenient to adjourn at that stage. He said that he had decided to take the case again at 10:30 A.M. on the next day, if that course would be convenient to the legal gentlemen concerned.

This being smoothly agreed, Mr. Berwick Law applied for bail on his client's behalf, and Sir Charles said, with an expressionless face, that it would be necessary for it to be of substantial amount: the defendant herself in £500, and two sureties, each of £1,000, to the satisfaction of the police.

Mr. Berwick Law said that there would be no difficulty about that, and it was within half an hour that the necessary formalities were completed, and Belle was free, for one night at least, to return to her hotel, where a good dinner in company of her sister and Reggie Tudor concluded a tiring day.

She ended it in good spirits enough, feeling that it had gone well, and that there would be more evidence of the right kind. But her ordeal was yet to come.

CHAPTER XLV.

Should She Have Said That?

WHATEVER hope or courage there may have been in the heart of the one most concerned, at the end of the first day's hearing, there was little confidence in her defence among the legal gentlemen who, either as gladiators or spectators, had observed its course.

The most, they thought, that the defence would succeed in establishing—which might be their utmost aim—was that the libel had not been uttered without plausible cause, or what, at least, might have been so considered by an illogical female brain.

In any—or almost any—event, committal for trial would be certain. There would, of course, be postponement, with the probability of final collapse, if the police should arrest Gilson before the day of the hearing would come; but surely, if they had any such intention, they would have done so already. Their inaction seemed alone sufficient to condemn the defendant.

And that being the general verdict upon the case when the defendant had been examined only under the friendly guidance of her own counsel, what was it likely to be when Bulfit had had his turn?

But Mr. Bulfit himself took a rather different view. "You know, Plumer," he said, "there's bound to be a committal. I've no doubt I can get you that. But I'm looking ahead. We can't afford to have any surprises sprung on us in this case. We want to draw out the defence to the full, and see how much ground they've got for behaving the way they have. I've never liked the case since I saw Jellipot's letter. He's got the reputation of being cautious as well as shrewd—"

"He may have thought he could sidetrack us on a question of privilege. It's being said that he feels he's more or less responsible for setting the young lady on."

"Well, he mayn't have been far wrong. I mean on the question of privilege. It would have been a new point. I've had it looked up thoroughly—just out of interest—and there's no precedent. Nothing

163

like it at all. But, if he did, it just shows we've got opponents we can't afford to treat lightly."

"I understand that Law's putting Jellipot into the box as soon as you've finished with Miss Reeves."

"Then we ought to know a bit more when we've done with him."

"Do you think Gilson really is Ames?"

"I don't know. At a guess, I should say not. But it was a queer business the way Jellipot put those questions, and the answers they got. Of course, they were leading questions, and the young woman may just have made up what she thought she was paid to say. While Ames can't be found, she'd know no one could prove her wrong. I daresay I can upset her. And Shole. And even if Gilson is Ames, it doesn't follow that anyone could prove it now. But his danger is that this case may develop in such a way that the police will be forced to prosecute, where they'd have preferred not to take the risk. Whether he's innocent or guilty, he's our client, and it's our business to save him from that.

"I won't go farther yet than to say that he made a good witness, and he's in no danger if they've really turned up all their best cards."

"They're bound to do that now. If anything isn't on the depositions—"

"Yes. Unless there's excuse. Leave to call new witnesses— there's always danger of that. We've got to make it as hard as we can for them to keep anything back. Well, it's time to go in now. We'll see how Miss Reeves shapes when she isn't being shown the way she's wanting to go." Saying this, he led the way back into court, where the magistrate had already taken his seat, and Belle, who had re-entered the dock, was guided again to the witness box for Mr. Bulfit to have his turn.

He began in a way which made it evident to those familiar with his methods that he was not intending to make her the subject of any violent attack.

"You have told us, Miss Reeves," he said, "that you were led to make these dreadful accusations against Mr. Gilson by something which was said to you by Mr. Jellipot, by the questions that he suggested you should put to Miss Butcher, and by the answers which they received. Is that a fair statement of the information on which you acted?"

"Yes. Except that there was Clara Shole as well."

"Have you ever discussed the subject with Clara Shole?"

"No."

"Then we may put her on one side. Those who gave you opinions, or what you accepted as information, were Mr. Jellipot and Miss Butcher?"

"Yes."

"Now please answer this question very carefully. Up to the night on which you uttered this libel in the dining room of the Regent Street Hotel, had Mr. Jellipot told you that he was sure that Mr. Gilson and Mr. Ames were the same man?"

"No, he hadn't gone as far as that."

"He had not. And did Miss Butcher go as far as that? Did she say that Mr. Gilson and Mr. Ames were the same man?"

"No. But she—"

"Never mind that. She either did or she did not, and your answer is no. Both Mr. Gilson and Mr. Ames must have attended frequently at Mr. Jellipot's office in connection with Briggs & Co.'s affairs?"

"Yes."

"And Miss Butcher was actually employed by Mr. Ames as manager of Briggs & Co., and afterwards by Mr. Gilson in a similar relationship?"

"Yes."

"So that either Mr. Jellipot or Miss Butcher must have had as good, if not even much better, opportunities than yourself of judging whether they were two different men?"

"They didn't say they were different men. I don't think Mr. Jellipot thought they were."

"But Miss Butcher did?"

"I don't know."

"Then on your own admission you made this libellous statement on no more foundation than what you had heard from two people, neither of whom drew any certain deduction from what they knew?"

Belle was evidently in no haste to answer this question. There was a moment of waiting silence before she spoke, but when the reply came it was not of denial, or of an evasive or argumentative kind. In her pleasantest tone (and we know that those tones could be very pleasant indeed), she answered: "Yes. I think that's just about how it was."

Mr. Bulfit, scarcely prepared for the readiness of this assent, did not therefore fail to put the further question which it invited.

"And you thought it right to make this criminal charge, with all its preposterous improbability—a charge for which the police themselves, whose public duty it is to deal with such matters, had evidently decided that there was no sufficient foundation—on no better basis than that?"

"It was just because the police wouldn't do anything that someone else had to."

"You consider that to be a sufficient reply?"

"I think that I took the one way by which the truth will come out, and that's what I meant to happen."

Mr. Bulfit's satisfaction at this admission, which went considerably beyond what he had expected to get, was somewhat reduced by a murmur of applause, slight and decorous, but no less significant for that, which broke out at the back of the court, and died instantly at the magistrate's admonitory word.

But he was not playing up to a jury now. Frankness such as that might win popular approval, but its legal effect would be no less when it should be on Miss Reeves' deposition, with a signature below it.

He sat down, with the feeling that he had done well.

"Any further questions, Mr. Berwick Law?" Sir Charles asked.

But Mr. Law said that he did not wish to re-examine. He recognised that what had been said could not easily be modified or withdrawn. And he was undecided as to whether he would wish it to be so.

He might have shared the doubt which was now on Muriel's mind as to whether Belle should have said that.

CHAPTER XLVI.

THE SECOND MORNING'S EVIDENCE

MR. JELLIPOT entered the witness box. It would not have occurred to him under easily conceivable circumstances to be less than meticulously accurate in his evidence, but, within that limit, there is a wide range of choice as to what any or may not be said.

He took the oath with distaste, not from religious scruple, but because its wording appeared to place him under an obligation which he did not intend, and would not have been allowed, to fulfil. If every witness were to speak the whole truth so far as it related to the cause of action, well, there would have to be fewer cases or more courts. But he told himself that the curious tautological wording was not to be taken literally. The intention of its undertaking was that the truth should be told without reserve or perversion, which he would certainly aim to do.

Having completed its inevitable preliminaries, and briefly covered his contacts with those concerned up to the date of the murder, the examination went on: "At what time did the idea that Ames and Gilson might be the same man first enter your mind?"

"Almost immediately afterwards. It appeared certain that Ames was the murderer, but I could neither observe nor imagine any adequate motive which he could have had. Neither could I see that Gilson could have any which could be considered adequate to a sane mind.

"Then, as I pondered the problem, I observed that, had they been the same man, the combined motive might be much stronger, and as I idly considered this, as a mere abstract theory, I recalled what had seemed to me a remarkable coincidence at the time, and might have appeared even more so had I given it more serious thought."

Mr. Jellipot went on to describe the incident of the gloved hand, and the cut which he had observed between Gilson's fingers, so remarkably similar to what he had seen on Ames's hand on the previous day. He continued: "At first I did not entertain the idea seriously. It appeared to be of a fantastic improbability. But I saw that it might be disproved, absolutely and at once, in many ways, and I began to look for such disproofs, and was somewhat intrigued to be unable to find them.

"I could neither recall nor hear of any certain occasion when the two men had been together, and while I was anticipating such an event, so that an absurd idea might be finally cast out of my mind, I heard of the disappearance of Ames.

"I then observed that, if my theory were right, Ames would not be found, and when the police failed to trace him I began—I think for the first time—to take the idea seriously.

"Considering it in that spirit, I observed that it could only have been possible if one of the two had been fundamentally disguised, and that, for physical reasons, that one must have been Ames.

"It was therefore easy to advise Miss Reeves that the path of certainty lay in making enquiries in the first place as to whether the movements and contacts of the two men had been such that their separate identity was assured, and otherwise whether Ames had been disguised, in particular by the padding of his clothes, and by wearing a wig.

"The results of those enquiries are matters on which I can give no direct testimony."

This statement had been made with the clarity natural to its author, and the deliberation necessary for its written record. Its effect on the intently silent court was such that it may be said that it was at this point that the defendant's case reached its maximum plausibility. Only Bulfit, militantly watchful, was unmoved as he made the rapid notes on which his cross-examination was to be founded.

"Mr. Jellipot," he began, in his most conversational manner—for Berwick Law asked no further questions, relying upon his later witnesses to build on a foundation so firmly laid—"you will agree that you are an exceptionally observant man?"

Mr. Jellipot considered this, and replied simply: "No."

"Yet on two occasions you observed a small cut in a particularly inconspicuous position, which was in no way related to the business you had on hand?"

"It is possible to exaggerate the inconspicuousness of the cut, to which my attention may, on the second occasion, have been abnormally directed by Mr. Gilson's reluctance to remove his glove."

"Yet, at that time, the idea of the identity of the two men did not enter your mind?"

"It was not a normal probability."

"We can agree there. You had had these two men at your office, not, naturally, together, but on near, if not actual consecutive days, and you had not been sufficiently observant to doubt, on any previous grounds, that they were the same?"

"No."

"Had you arrived at a settled conviction of their identity at any time up to the day on which this libel was uttered?"

"No."

"So that Miss Reeves had no authority from you for the assertion she made?"

"We may conclude that her judgment was sounder and less halting than mine."

"Or we may conclude something quite different. Having this suspicion in your mind, you naturally informed the police?"

"I did."

"And they doubtless made their own enquiries?"

"Doubtless."

"And they have done nothing?"

"They have not yet arrested Gilson."

"You appreciate the significance of that? And yet you are reluctant to reject this fantastic theory, for which it appears you are solely responsible?"

"It is not a matter on which reluctance could have any weight."

"You find no difficulty in accepting this incredible theory?"

"I cannot accept 'incredible'. But I have found a great difficulty."

"What is that?"

"Gilson appears to me to differ from Ames in speech and thought. It has seemed to me to be a genuine difference, which I cannot explain."

"Which, if your idea were an error, is just what might be expected?"

"Yes."

"Yet even that is not enough to cause you to abandon this perverse idea?"

"No. I have deliberately concluded that Gilson and Ames are the same man."

"And it is that opinion, obstinately held—against contrary observation which you cannot entirely exclude from your own mind—which has brought us here?"

"I agree that the primary responsibility is mine, but it was for that reason that I gave your client an opportunity of proceeding against myself."

Mr. Bulfit sat down, feeling that he had got some admissions from Mr. Jellipot which would look well on the depositions, but not entirely pleased that he had given opportunity for the last answer, nor entirely satisfied that he had not been led on to do it. But he had a cautious fear that if he should go further he might fare worse, and he knew that there must be other witnesses to come who should be easier prey.

Mr. Jellipot left the box, and it was at this point that Berwick Law made a tactical error in calling Reggie Tudor, though its result was one which the most experienced advocate might not have been reasonably expected to foresee.

Actually, Mr. Jellipot's arrangement had been that Bessie Butcher should be the next witness, to be followed by Clara Shole, Reggie Tudor being kept in reserve to refute any lies such as Bessie might be quite likely to tell.

But Berwick Law thought that the girl might be more disposed to follow the path of rectitude if she had just listened to a veracious narrative, and he wished to obtain her evidence in a form which would relieve him from the necessity of recalling the defendant to give conflicting evidence of that second interview, at which Reggie had not been present.

These may seem to be conclusive reasons, and it may also be said that the event would most probably have been the same at a later stage, unless Reggie's evidence had been entirely omitted. Anyway, so it was.

And Reggie gave his evidence well. He told of the patient enquiries he had made to ascertain the daily habits of Ames, and he was explicit that neither Mr. Jellipot nor Miss Reeves had desired him to discover facts to support the theory of the identity of the two men, but only to ascertain what the facts were.

He made it clear also that the money which the defendant had offered to Miss Butcher had been no more than an inducement to answer Mr. Jellipot's questions frankly, without any stipulation as to what those answers should be.

At the conclusion of Mr. Law's examination, the magistrate adjourned the court for a luncheon interval, giving both sides the brief respite which enables the course of the conflict to be considered, and fresh dispositions made.

CHAPTER XLVII.

THE CASE GOES BADLY FOR BELLE

MR. BULFIT, eating a good lunch, such as was easy, in those pre-war days, for affluent legal gentlemen to command, considered a position with which he was not entirely satisfied. He was not perturbed, for he reckoned that the less satisfactory (and most essential) witnesses were still to come. But he felt it to be a battle in which he could not afford to overlook any advantage, however slight, or fail to probe for any possible weakness which might lie behind the formidable façade which the defence were erecting in support of their audacious plea.

Reflecting thus, he observed that the evidence of the last witness had stopped at the first interview with Bessie Butcher. Had he done nothing subsequently? It seemed unlikely. If so, it was to be omitted from the depositions, with the evident inference that it had been of no assistance to the defence. Was it equally certain that it would be of no use to him? It could do no harm to enquire.

So when the court resumed, and Reggie Tudor went back to the witness box, Mr. Jellipot (who had been observing with a mixture of satisfaction and curiosity that the other Reggie, who had not been in court during the morning, was now seated beside his wife) was roused to a different consciousness by hearing Mr. Bulfit's question: "You have given the court a very full account of the investigations you made on the instructions of Mr. Jellipot, or at the instigation of Miss Reeves—it was not clear which—up to your interview with Miss Butcher. Will you please continue the narrative?"

"I didn't see Miss Butcher again."

"I didn't ask you to say what you didn't do. Did your investigation cease abruptly with that interview?"

"I made some enquiries in other directions."

"What were they?"

"I enquired as to whether Mr. Ames had any address in the neighbourhood of Antrobus Road."

"Why?"

"Because we thought there must be somewhere near there at which he got rid of his disguise."

"Why?"

"Because of the short time after Mr. Ames left Antrobus Road that Mr. Gilson was in Smith's Terrace."

The magistrate interposed: "You mean on the morning of the murder?"

"Yes."

"Well, go on, Mr. Bulfit."

"And, of course, you found that there was no such place?"

"I did not find that there was."

"So I should have supposed. And in the absence of such a place the whole theory of the identity of the two men falls to the ground?"

Reggie Tudor was inexperienced as a witness, but he had not passed his intermediate examination without having learnt something of the laws of evidence. So far, he may be said to have been hustled along a road he was reluctant to tread, at a pace which he could not check. But now he made a desperate effort to resist the pressure of the assault.

"That," he said, "is a matter of argument, not of fact."

"On the contrary, it is a matter of fact, not of argument."

Mr. Berwick Law was on his feet, to the succour of his harassed witness. "I suggest," he said, causing a ripple of amusement to pass over the tense watchfulness of the crowded court, "that it is a matter for argument whether it be a matter of argument or of fact."

Sir Charles Rentoul's quiet authoritative voice interposed. "Mr. Bulfit," he said, "we appear to be upon ground which was not traversed by your opening statement, and which is outside the range of any previous evidence we have had. I should be glad to understand what your argument is."

"It is scarcely my argument," Mr. Bulfit replied cautiously, "it is a difficulty which the defence appear to have observed for themselves, and on which they had made enquiries, with results which they had no desire to communicate to the court. It is evidently a question of when or how Ames could have become Gilson on the morning of the murder with sufficient celerity to provide the police with a satisfactory alibi."

The magistrate, being, in the absence of a jury, almost the only man there who had a single-minded desire to discover whatever the truth should be, saw that there might be a matter of vital importance here, which no legal tactics of either side should be allowed to obscure.

"It appears to me," he said, "that the issue which has been raised in the case may render the nature of Mr. Gilson's alibi of different, if not of greater, importance than it would otherwise be, and I should be much surprised if the police have not fully considered its implications, before deciding upon the course which the interests of justice required. Are you calling any police evidence, Mr. Berwick Law?"

Mr. Law, who had only intended to do so if it should become desirable to have the statements of Bessie Butcher and Clara Shole produced, replied at once that he should be calling Chief Inspector Combridge, who had been in charge of the investigation; and Sir Charles invited Mr. Bulfit to continue his cross-examination. But Mr. Bulfit knew when to let well alone. He said that he had no further questions to ask.

Reggie Tudor stepped down, and the court stirred to a new interest as Miss Elizabeth Butcher was invited to take his place.

CHAPTER XLVIII.

MISS BUTCHER CAN HOLD HER OWN

MISS BUTCHER, having to take part in a public performance, had dressed herself with unusual care. She was nervous, but only to that degree which gives alertness to the movements both of the limbs and the mind. She would have only men with whom to deal, of which no girl has need to be greatly afraid in a duel of verbal wits. The only woman arrayed against her was in the dock, which did not say much for hers. Clara Shole had also to be remembered. She was a friend, of course. But to be trusted? Well, hardly anyone would be as foolish as that. Anyhow, if Miss Butcher could not protect herself with her own tongue, it would be the first time that that active member had failed her at any need.

She had no wish to shield Gilson in any way, a feeling of active malice towards him being even stronger than her resentment against those who have promised her she should not be called upon to give public evidence, and then forced her to do so. But her first intention was to keep her own reputation clear of any illicit association with the fleeing murderer Ames, to which she thought she would be equal. So she took the oath, and gave her name and address (a silly business, for they knew it already, but men are like that), and began to give wary answers to Mr. Berwick Laws' pleasantly-modulated voice, addressing her with a politeness which she found it gratifying to hear.

"Now, Miss Butcher, you have heard the accounts which Miss Reeves and Mr. Tudor have given of their interview with you at your room in Puller Street. Were they substantially correct?"

"I expect they were, more or less. I didn't listen that close."

Sir Charles Rentoul said: "Wait a minute, Mr. Law." He turned to Bessie to ask: "You tell the court that you did not listen to evidence which so closely concerned yourself?"

Bessie's eyes flickered before the inscrutable experienced ones they met, but she answered boldly enough: "I said not that close."

"Then that evidence had better be read over to you before we proceed further."

This being done, Berwick Law repeated his previous question: "Do you admit the accuracy of that evidence?"

"I daresay it is. I don't remember that well."

"But you don't wish to contradict anything?"

"I don't see why I should. It's not that important to me."

Sir Charles interposed again: "Miss Butcher, I suppose you realise that this is a matter of extreme seriousness for both the parties concerned? I must ask you to do your utmost to answer the questions you are asked fully and accurately."

"That's why, if I don't remember, I'm not saying I do."

The reply was almost pert, but was not spoken aggressively, and it was reasonable, if her difficulty were sincere. But was her memory so bad?

Berwick Law, deciding that this witness must be attacked more sharply than he had first intended, said: "You're not being paid so much for your evidence now as you were then?"

"I wasn't paid to say things, if you mean that, any more than I'm being paid now."

"But you were paid?"

"They paid me for saying I didn't know, just like they did when I did."

"And you did know that Ames padded his clothes?"

"Yes, he did."

"Much?"

"I didn't see that close."

"When did you observe that?"

"When he took his coat off, when it was hot last summer."

"You mean at the works?"

"Yes, of course."

Bessie had been prepared for these questions. She knew that she had not only admitted that knowledge to Miss Reeves. It was set down in her statement to the police. She was prepared for the next question also, and for its indignant denial.

"And you observed the same thing when you visited Mr. Ames' flat?"

"No, I didn't. It wasn't likely I should."

"But you did visit him there—more than once?"

"I went twice to take things from the office he wanted there. I didn't stay enough to see anything, if you mean that."

"I didn't mean anything. I want you to tell the court what you know yourself."

"Well, I've done that."

Mr. Law paused, in some doubt of whether it would be wise to go further. He bent round to Mr. Jellipot to ask: "Anything else I ought to put to her?"

"No. I think not. Let Bulfit have her."

They knew she had already refused to identify Ames with Gilson. The more they brought out the degree of her intimacy with Ames, the more significant—against their own case—that refusal might appear to be. And they had heard her angry assertion that the bribes that Arabella had given her had not been dependant upon the nature of her replies. That was one thing they had wished to have.

Apart from that, Bulfit would be bound to ask the questions they left, and there might be no loss in that. So Mr. Berwick Law sat down, and Mr. Bulfit rose, well aware that he was venturing on a slippery path, but with the confidence that successful practice will give.

"Miss Butcher," he asked, "is it a fact that, when Mr. Tudor and Miss Reeves saw you, you denied that Mr. Ames padded his clothes?"

"No, I said I'd rather not say anything."

"And two days after, you saw Miss Reeves again on your own suggestion, and were paid five pounds for saying that you knew that he padded his clothes?"

"Yes, I'd altered my mind. Anyone can."

"Yes. But why?"

"I thought it was silly not to say, when she'd pay that."

"And you had been dismissed from your employment in the meantime?"

"Yes. But what's that got to do with it?"

"That is what we are trying to find out. Why had you been dismissed?"

"Mr. Gilson wouldn't give me a rise."

"That might be a reason why you should have left. It was no reason why he should dismiss you?"

"Well, he took it that way."

"Why do you think he did that?"

"Because he's mean. He wasn't like Mr. Ames at all."

"You saw Mr. Ames daily for a long period, and after that you saw Mr. Gilson with the same frequency, and you say they were not like one another at all?"

"I meant about being mean."

"But it would be equally true in other ways?"

"Yes. Lots."

"And, after Mr. Gilson had dismissed you, you were not very friendly to him?"

"There wouldn't be much sense in that, would there?"

"Possibly not. And so you wouldn't mind annoying him any way you could?"

"I didn't do anything, if you mean that."

"You knew that answering Miss Reeves' questions the way you did might cause him to have some annoyance from the police, if it meant nothing more than that?"

"I didn't see why it should."

"Well…you know now. So it comes to this: Miss Reeves asked you whether Mr. Ames padded his clothes, and offered you five pounds to answer, and you very properly refused to have anything to do with such nonsense, but after Mr. Gilson had dismissed you, you decided to answer, and say he did?"

"It wasn't because of that."

"Whatever the reasons were, that was what happened?"

"Yes. About that."

"And then you took another five pounds for saying that you didn't know whether Mr. Ames wore a wig, but giving the name of another girl who might be willing to say he did?"

"They didn't pay me for that."

"I didn't suggest that they did. It was all part of an attack which was to be made on Mr. Gilson, who had dismissed you the day before?"

"I didn't know it was for that."

"But you wouldn't mind helping an attack on Mr. Gilson?"

"I didn't see that it was. I didn't think Mr. Ames did the murder. He wasn't the sort who would. I think it was Mr. Gilson more likely than not."

Mr. Bulfit, met by this unexpected retort, objected sharply: "I didn't ask what you think, and I—" but he checked himself as the magistrate interposed with more severity than he often spoke: "Miss Butcher, I must ask you to confine yourself to answering the questions, and to facts which are within your own knowledge." He directed that the reply should not be recorded in the depositions.

After that, Mr. Bulfit said he had nothing further to ask, and Mr. Berwick Law declined his opportunity of re-examination. He was certain that she was lying about the occasions when she had visited Ames' flat, and probably on other essential matters, but she was his witness. What was the sense of discrediting her further? She had been unwilling to say that Ames and Gilson were the same man, and even if she could be persuaded to waver from that position now, she had shown an animus towards Gilson which would discredit such an alteration of attitude. The case was certainly not going well. But could that be helped?

Bessie Butcher stepped down from the box, with a comfortable feeling that she had done no good to anybody, and that they'd got what they deserved for having shown so little consideration for her, and Clara Shole took her place.

CHAPTER XLIX.

Clara Is Quite Sure

CLARA SHOLE was not drunk. She was, indeed, in a state of average sobriety by the standard of recent weeks, but she had been imbibing. She was in an excitable condition, caring much less about her reputation than Bessie Butcher—as to which it may be said that she had somewhat less to lose—but resolved to use the occasion for the unveiling of Henry Gilson, of whose identity with the murderous Ames she had no doubt at all, having cultivated an increased assurance from day to day, or rather from night to night, as she had asserted it in the Turk's Head bar.

Here, at last, was a witness who would support the defence in no ambiguous or half-hearted manner. But Mr. Berwick Law viewed her with apprehension, if not with fear. He felt that this was where he must stand or fall, and the too-willing witness is as dangerous as the one who is too-cautious in all he says.

She took the oath, and gave her name and other preliminary particulars with fluent readiness, though her words were not always easy to catch. Then the examination began: "Did you know your manager, Mr. Robert Ames, well?"

"Rather."

Sir Charles Rentoul: "You mean rather well?"

Mr. Berwick Law: "May we say that you knew him intimately?"

"I'd say I did."

The film-learned Americanism did not please the magistrate any better than her previous answer. "It would be better," he said, "if you would reply either yes or no."

"Yes."

The defending counsel continued: "You knew him intimately. And did you see Mr. Gilson from day to day until you left the employment of Briggs & Co. at your own wish?"

179

"That was it...yes."

"Have you any doubt that Robert Ames and Henry Gilson are the same man?"

"I'd take my dying oath as Gilson's the man."

"You have taken an oath a few minutes ago," the magistrate interposed again. "Do I understand you to say that you are sure that Robert Ames and Henry Gilson are the same?"

"Yes."

"Very well. The answer is yes. Go on, Mr. Law."

"Before the murder of Mr. Briggs, did you have any reason to think that Robert Ames disguised himself in any way?"

"I knew what I saw."

"What did you see?"

"I saw his wig on the stairs."

"On what stairs?"

"Where he lived. When he was coming down from the flat."

"Any other disguise?"

"He used to fill up his clothes to make himself look a fat man."

"How did you know that?"

"Well, I did."

Sir Charles: "Did you see it yourself?"

"As plain as I see you now."

"Never mind how you see me. The answer is clearly yes. Go on, Mr. Law."

"Did you observe any other mode of disguise?"

"No. But that doesn't say there wasn't any I didn't see."

"Your answer is no. But did you recognise Henry Gilson as Robert Ames would be without his wig, and without his shape being altered?"

"Yes. That's about it."

"You say yes. Now look round the court. Do you see Mr. Henry Gilson?"

"Yes. Over there."

"Do you see Robert Ames?"

"Yes. He's the same man."

"Thank you. I think that will be all."

Mr. Law sat down, and Mr. Bulfit got up, with the motion of one who felt that his time had come.

"Now, Miss Shole," he began briskly, "perhaps you'll tell the court when you first became so sure that Robert Ames and Henry Gilson are the same man?"

"I've never had much doubt about that."

"You were not sure when you left Briggs & Co.?"

"That was just why I left."

"And of course you informed the police?"

"I told them about the wig and the rest."

"But that wasn't the same thing at all. If Ames disguised himself, that doesn't prove he was Henry Gilson, any more than it proves he was you or me. And you didn't tell the police anything until long after—in fact, till they came to you. Isn't that the truth?"

"Of course, it was when they asked me."

"But why not before?"

"It wasn't that much business of mine."

"Not if you knew that a murderer for whom the police were searching was with you from day to day?"

"They might see for themselves without asking me."

"If they didn't know that Ames had been disguised, you couldn't expect them to do that. But I am going to suggest that there is quite a different explanation. I want you to think carefully before you answer. You'll remember it's written down. *Didn't you tell Chief-Inspector Combridge, long after, that you couldn't say that Henry Gilson was the same man as Robert Ames? Didn't you sign a statement to that effect?*"

"That was only to the police, if I did."

"*Only* to the police! Do you mean that you said and signed the very contrary to what you knew to be true?"

"I didn't say he wasn't the same. I only didn't say that I knew. That was just for the police. I didn't want any trouble with them. I didn't swear anything."

"But you are on oath now. I suggest to you that you are doing yourself a very grave injustice. I suggest that you would have told the police at once if you had known, or even thought, that the two men were one. Haven't you been getting more sure of it every time that you've repeated it night by night in the Turk's Head bar?"

Clara was looking sulky now, and her voice rose to a shriller pitch, as she answered: "I've only said what I know. Anyone can do that."

In saying this, she was asserting little more, however ignorantly, than the legal gentlemen who heard her knew to be true.

By English law, anyone who has nothing to lose, and is therefore in no danger by civil action, can say almost anything of a slanderous kind with impunity, however serious it may be. Had Belle merely spoken her accusation, Gilson's remedy would have been by civil process only, though she had shouted it in public places a dozen times—unless by doing so she had committed an incidental breach of the peace of a less serious kind, for which she might have been moderately fined.

But Mr. Bulfit did not turn aside to discuss with Clara the mystery of English legal distinction between spoken and written words. He repeated his accusation in what became less like a question than a denunciatory speech, so that Sir Charles hesitated as to whether he ought not to interpose.

"I suggest to you that this monstrous, poisonous, utterly preposterous idea that a man could have been living two lives, different in manner, different in appearance, different in character, year after year, and latterly meeting the same people, did not originate in your own mind, but was first put to you by Mr. Tudor or Miss Reeves, when you naturally rejected it for the falsehood which you knew it to be; that it was suggested to you again by the police, when you rejected it once again; and that it is only at a later date, when you have been led by vanity to say more than you meant, and to exaggerate it from day to day, that you have adopted a theory which started in other minds. So that you have said it because it was imagined by others, and these people now ask us to believe it is said by you. Is not that just what has occurred?"

Clara said sullenly: "No, it isn't. It isn't like that at all." But her eyes were downcast, and there was no conviction in her tone.

There were few who heard, either of the general public or of the representatives of the law, who did not see that a liar was in the box, let the truth be what it might, and of that the remaining doubt was not much. There might be sympathy for the girl in the dock, whose foolish impetuosity and generous indignation at her uncle's murder had brought her to such jeopardy. But did not her obstinate persistence in asserting that which was so unlikely in itself, and failed of proof so utterly, deserve as much as it was likely to get?

Surely the major sympathy should be for the man so falsely and so terribly accused of that which, by its nature, was not easy to put aside.

The witness stood hesitantly, not knowing whether her ordeal were over. She made a movement to leave the box, and the usher motioned her back.

Sir Charles was looking at Berwick Law, but that gentleman, who had the right to re-examine, was in earnest conversation with Mr. Jellipot.

Had they decided to advise the defendant to withdraw a plea which they could no longer hope to sustain? It seemed to most of those who looked on to be a most probable thing.

So the magistrate may have thought, as he sat patiently silent, ignoring the discourtesy of the delay. It seemed to those who watched that the solicitor was urging the barrister to a course that he was reluctant to take, but at last he shrugged his shoulders, and rose to apologise.

"Never mind that; Mr. Law," Sir Charles answered. "What I have been waiting to say is that if you wish to re-examine the witness, we will go on. But it has become evident that we cannot finish today—you have still the police evidence to call. And, if you have no more questions to ask, it will be a convenient time at which to adjourn, so soon as the deposition is signed."

"I have no further questions to ask this witness, but I have to request that the prosecutor be recalled. There are one or two questions which may be put to him at this stage, and which I am anxious not to defer."

Mr. Bulfit rose quickly: "I must object to that, unless the cross-examination of the prosecutor is to be completed in a regular manner."

"Then I am afraid I must rule against you, Mr. Bulfit. The case appears to me to be one in which I must allow all reasonable latitude to the defence."

"It is extremely irregular."

"Not necessarily. You must take the risk, Mr. Law, that I may direct you that the cross-examination shall be completed before other witnesses are taken."

Berwick Law said nothing to that, and Henry Gilson was recalled to the box.

CHAPTER L.

Who Is John Burton?

"MR. GILSON, I believe you know Mr. John Burton?"

Henry Gilson looked for a moment as though it were a question he had not expected, and introduced matters to which he could not instantly adjust his mind, but after that he answered readily: "Yes."

"And he was also known to Robert Ames?"

"Not to my knowledge. I know nothing about that at all."

"You paid him large sums?"

"I shouldn't call them large. Some of them were considerable."

"What were they for?"

"Stamps."

"What sort of man was he?"

"I have no idea."

"I mean in appearance."

"I could not answer that. I never saw him."

"Never?"

"Never at all. The business I had with him was by correspondence."

"Where did he live?"

"I am not sure that I could tell you from memory. It was a London address."

Counsel glanced down to a half-sheet of note paper which Mr. Jellipot had given him.

"I will try to refresh your memory. Was it in Haslett Street?"

"Yes. I should say you are right."

"Perhaps he is still there?"

"How could I possibly answer that?"

"He was there less than three months ago?"

"I know of no reason to doubt it."

"If your last transaction with him was within that time?"

184

"Then he was obviously there. That is, if he wrote from that address."

"Your transactions with him would be recorded in the books at your Strand office?"

"Naturally."

"And there would be correspondence there to confirm the nature of your transactions?"

"I have no doubt that there is."

"Will you have these documentary evidences in court at the next hearing?"

"I see no earthly reason why I should disclose private business affairs which can have no possible connection with the case."

"But if you are directed by the court to do so?"

"Naturally I should obey such a direction."

Mr. Bulfit rose.

"I must make the strongest protest—" he began, and was interrupted by the magistrate's quiet authoritative voice: "You need not concern yourself, Mr. Bulfit, with any fear that I should require the production of such documents without their relevancy being clearly shown. But there can be no harm in your having them here. I am sure I can rely upon Mr. Berwick Law not to abuse the indulgence of the court."

Mr. Law, who had resumed his seat, rose again.

"I propose to call evidence, after the hearing of which Mr. Gilson may be in no doubt of the importance of showing the nature of his transactions with the gentleman whom he never met."

"You appreciate, Mr. Law, that this court cannot be used for the purpose of making an attack upon the character of the prosecutor, except it be clearly related to the plea of justification of the libel with which we are dealing?"

Mr. Law said that he fully appreciated that, and Sir Charles said that he had confidence in that assurance. The court would adjourn until 10:30 A.M. tomorrow.

Mr. Plumer called his client aside as the court rose: "You'd better tell us what this means," he said. "It's all Greek to me."

Mr. Gilson was unperturbed, but he said he had no explanation at all. Burton was a man he had never met in his life. He had bought stamps from him. More than once or twice? Yes, quite frequently. But that was no crime, so far as Mr. Gilson had ever heard.

Mr. Plumer looked unconvinced. "There must," he said, "be more in it than that. Well, you'd better bring the books and correspondence along."

It was Mr. Bulfit's view also that there must be "more in it than that." But what could it be? He said that, if anything awkward were sprung on them, they would ask for a substantial adjournment. Sir Charles couldn't refuse that.

Mr. Jellipot had drawn Sir Reginald Crowe into conversation with Berwick Law. Sir Reginald was saying: "You won't get him here unless you subpoena him. And he won't forgive me for that. Not in a hundred years. Especially if it doesn't come off."

Mr. Berwick Law saw difficulties. He said: "You'll find that Sir Charles won't order them to say anything unless we show him at the start what we're aiming to prove."

Sir Reginald said they ought to be equal to getting some hint to him before ten-thirty tomorrow. Berwick Law looked shocked. He knew that such things do happen, and will again. But they are not spoken of to non-legal ears.

He went back to chambers to fortify himself with any useful precedent of procedure his books might give, while Mr. Jellipot hurried off to the office from which subpoenas are issued.

Belle, who must be bailed out for a second night, remained in the dock. Everyone seemed to have forgotten her.

CHAPTER LI.

MR. JELLIPOT TAKES A RISK

EVELYN said: "Do you mind if we come back to the hotel with you, and all have dinner together there? I don't know how your Reggie will behave after the time he had in the witness box, but mine's in such a temper over what Mr. Jellipot made him do that I'm afraid to go home."

Arabella (released from the dock at last) smiled at this assertion of marital misery, but added more seriously: "I'm sorry I've been the cause of his doing something he dislikes so much. I am really grateful to him. But I believe I ought to thank you as much as anyone. I can't think why you've been so good to me."

"Oh, you mean going bail? There's nothing in that. Anyone could see you didn't mean running away. I expect Sir Charles would have done it himself if there'd been any real need."

As Evelyn uttered this dubious imagination, Sir Reginald joined them, showing no visible evidence of the state of mind his wife attributed to him. He shook hands cordially with Arabella. "Had rather a racketing day, I'm afraid," he said. "But I shouldn't wonder if things look better tomorrow. Coming, Evelyn?"

"No. You are coming with us. We're all going to have dinner together. We're only waiting for Mr. Jellipot—and, of course, Mr. Tudor—now."

"Oh, are we? I should have thought Jellipot would have had the sense to keep further away."

"He doesn't know yet, but I felt I would be safer with legal protection and a few witnesses."

"Well, I wouldn't say you're far wrong. What Wickham's going to say when he gets that subpoena tonight—"

At this moment, Mr. Jellipot came up, followed by Reggie Tudor. If the solicitor had any fear of Sir Reginald's wrath, he concealed it under his usual aspect of quiet geniality.

187

"I suppose," the banker began, "you've done the dirty work on Wickham and Bailey-Wren? And that's what's making you look like a cat that's just emptied the canary's cage?"

"The two gentlemen will certainly be required to be in court tomorrow unless they're sleeping out tonight," Mr. Jellipot replied placidly.

"But they're not summoned till eleven-thirty, to give them time to get what they are required to produce. I shall have to tell Law to go slow with Combridge, and keep him in the box till we see one of them walk in."

Arabella said: "As I'm the one most concerned, perhaps someone will let me know what's been happening a bit more exactly than I do now."

"Mr. Jellipot's the best one to tell you that," Evelyn answered; "and the best time will be when we're having dinner, so you'd better all come along now."

As no one showed any reluctance to accept this decision, for even Belle felt that appetite must take precedence of curiosity, the whole half-dozen (for Muriel was naturally at her sister's side) crowded into a single taxi, and it was scarcely half an hour later that they were seated round a table on which an early dinner was being served.

"And now," Evelyn said, as she presided, after some persuasion, at a dinner at which she was hostess, though it was in the Misses Reeves' suite, "perhaps you'll tell us what we've got to look forward to tomorrow."

Mr. Jellipot was serious in his reply: "I wish I were more sure of that than I am. I suppose we shall either bring out enough evidence to secure Gilson's arrest, or be in a worse position than we were before."

"You couldn't be much worse than you are now, if you ask me," Sir Reginald said cheerfully, "and if it weren't for Miss Belle, I'd wish you the worst luck that you ever had. But anyway, there can't be anything worse than a committal tomorrow, and you'll get another month, more or less, to see what you can hatch up next."

"Of course," Belle said, "I know all about what Reggie was doing. It's what it's led to—"

"It's led," the elder Reginald interrupted, "to the chairman of the St. James's Bank, and a respectable bank manager of my own, being hauled into court to disclose the confidential affairs of a customer who may have nothing to do with the case, and against whom there's not a shred of evidence that he ever did anything wrong.

"It'll probably mean my getting boycotted in the city, so that I have to resign for the good of the bank, and take to drink, or collecting some of Gilson's stamps—"

"I hope not," Evelyn interrupted, without appearing much concerned at the fate which threatened her husband's future. "You spend quite enough on stamps now."

Her thoughts wandered for a moment to the theft of a collection, on which he had spent she did not know how much, and received £80,000 as inadequate compensation from an insurance company,[1] but returned quickly to the subject which was on all their minds as she went on: "But I don't believe Mr. Jellipot would have asked you to do anything which would be likely to have such dreadful consequences."

"Don't you? He'd murder his own grandmother, if it were necessary to get one of his clients out of a mess."

"And I'm sure you wouldn't do such a thing, if he went down on his knees."

"I didn't do it for him; I did it because you pestered me day and night, and I thought, if we get ruined in consequence, you'll get just what you deserve."

"Well," Evelyn replied, without any visible sign of dismay at the prospect of impending ruin, "I've often known you act from a worse motive than that."

Belle listened to these marital exchanges with a trouble in her mind which her eyes showed, for it was hard to judge what core of seriousness they might contain, and it was evident that whatever risks had been taken were intended to get her out of the mess to which her own rashness had led; but this time, at least, she gave no occasion for her sister's frequent protest, for she said nothing at all. It was Muriel who was next to speak.

"If Mr. Jellipot would tell us what's really happened—" she suggested, and her words brought a general silence, until the solicitor began the explanation with customary deliberation.

"I think we have all recognized," he said, "that one of the greatest difficulties in accepting the theory that Gilson and Ames are the same man has been that of reconciling the fact that he must have left the scene of the murder in the person of Ames—as Mrs. Collis asserted, and as Mrs. Fishwick corroborated—within so very short a time before he appeared in Smith's Terrace in the garb and aspect of the other man.

---

[1]This happened before the date of its recovery—see *The Murder in Bethnal Square.*

"Of course, this difficulty would disappear if the evidence of Blake could be put aside. It is absolutely unsupported, and the possibility that it might be a false alibi has never been absent from my mind, nor, of course, from that of Inspector Combridge.

"Indeed, it has been the knowledge that he regarded it with particular suspicion ever since he has accepted the possibility that our theory may be correct, which has enabled me to put it aside in the confidence that he has been doing everything possible to explore that angle of the matter.

"Unfortunately for us—as he told me only yesterday—all his enquiries have supported the conclusion that there was no collusion between Gilson and Blake, and that the latter described what had occurred substantially as he believed it to have been.

"This has thrown us back entirely upon the alternative possibility—that of Ames having had some place of resort in the neighbourhood of Antrobus Road where he could make such alterations in his personal appearance as the transformation required, and with the celerity which practice would be likely to give.

"With the object of discovering such a place, Mr. Tudor, as most of us already know, has been making the most exhaustive enquiries that the short time at our disposal has allowed, and, in doing this, he has had invaluable assistance from the principal house agents in the district, with whom I am fortunately on very friendly terms.

"Road by road, for some surrounding distance, we have considered the tenancies of premises of every description, and, after eliminating such as were beyond suspicion, have made such enquiries as did not, indeed, lead to any discovery such as would be useful to us, but enabled us to list a residuum among which, if it exists at all, the place of which we are in search must certainly be.

"In this position, and with the remaining time at our disposal (at least, before the prospect of a committal has to be faced) becoming desperately short, a possibility occurred to me which could only be probed through the co-operation of the banks concerned.

"I knew that Ames had a banking account with the Kilburn branch of the London & Northern, and that Gilson banked with the St. James's in Piccadilly, and it occurred to me that if any premises were utilised for the purpose of transition from the real Gilson to the disguised Ames, they would almost certainly have been rented in an assumed name. If that were so, a bank account in the assumed name would be probable, and if we postulate its existence, it becomes almost certain that it would be fed by cheques from either Gilson's or

Ames' accounts, and probable that it would be used as a medium for transferring money from the one personality to the other.

"I therefore, with the assistance of the house agents, and Mr. Tudor's diligent enquiries, had a list made of all the tenants, of whatever kind, of whom we were not entirely unsuspicious, and supplied it to Sir Reginald, with a request that Ames' account might be examined to ascertain whether he had at any time during recent years drawn cheques to any of the names appearing thereon, or received credits from them; and I asked him to use his influence with the chairman of the St. James's to examine Gilson's account to the same purpose.

"I was quite sure that Sir Reginald would not allow considerations of banking etiquette to result"—Mr. Jellipot turned to Arabella with a smile as he said this—"in your being wrongly convicted on such a charge; and I anticipated that he would first make discreet enquiries at his own branch, and, if they should supply affirmative evidence that our suspicions are not without foundation, that he would then go further and ask the proprietor—Mr. Evans Wickham is almost literally that—of the St. James's Bank to make a similar search at their end. It is evident that this has been done, and that the result is that cheques to or from Mr, John Burton, who is one of those on our list, have been recorded on both accounts."

"Which means," Sir Reginald interposed, "that Gilson *is* Ames, and that you ought to have seen the last of that dirty dock a good while before this time tomorrow. Unfortunately, it means also—"

For perhaps the first time in his mentally well-disciplined life, Mr. Jellipot interrupted another speaker with abrupt irritation.

"Unfortunately, it doesn't mean anything of the kind. And, if it did, we might still be far from the legal proof which the case requires.

"The first question is whether there is a John Burton or not. There'll be an officer of the court searching for him, and with the right sort of paper to bring him to court tomorrow. If he exists, it may be favourable to us to this limited extent, that no difficulty of procedure can prevent our putting him in the box, and we shall be able to get his account of his transactions with both Ames and Gilson—probably before Gilson has been able to make contact with him.

"But even so, we shall be on very dangerous ground. If he can give even a plausible account of what those transactions were, whether false or true, it won't do us any good, for the time being at least. Actually, it may do us harm. It would be very unlikely that it would prevent a committal. Our hope would be in what further we might be able to discover before the trial.

"But our better hope, and what I am sufficiently sanguine to anticipate as the greater probability, is that Burton does not exist, which we may guess, but which may be much harder to prove. And that may even increase the immediate difficulty of upsetting any explanations Gilson may give, or ignorance he may profess.

"We may succeed in establishing that the real or mythical Burton had financial transactions with both Gilson and Ames, but if Gilson can maintain that his own were in connection with his ordinary business—which it may be most difficult to disprove—we shall have done no more than arouse a vague suspicion. It is no crime for him to have had transactions with a man who also had transactions with Ames, however curious or improbable a coincidence it may be, and we may find that Rentoul will pull us up before we get even that far."

"I think," Sir Reginald said, "you're making it sound a damned lot worse than it is. Of course, you're sunk if the transactions are really about stamps with a real man, and there's no more in it than that. But is it likely? And now you know where to look, why shouldn't the police have a poke at that Haslett Street room? They might find the whole outfit there, wig and all, and what would Gilson say then?"

Mr. Jellipot answered literally: "He would probably say that he knew nothing about it, and what were Burton's actions to do with him?"

"The fact is, Jellipot," the banker retorted, "you got Evelyn to persuade me to do something of which I shall be ashamed as long as I live, and now it's done you're trying to make out that it's not worth a damn. And if that's the truth—"

How Sir Reginald would have concluded this accusation, or whether Mr. Jellipot (as is likely) would have been equal to its reply, must remain unknown, for at this moment the telephone rang, and Muriel, who took the call, said: "Belle, it's Inspector Combridge. He's asking for you. He'd better come up, hadn't he?"

"Yes, of course."

"It looks," Sir Reginald surmised, "as though they've been quicker than they usually are. I expect they've raided Haslett Street, and got Gilson locked up by now."

But the news that Combridge brought was widely different from that.

"We've found out something queer," he said, "which we certainly didn't expect. I don't know where it leads, but I thought you ought to know. I rang up," he added, turning to Mr. Jellipot, "your home phone, and when I heard that you weren't expected till late, I thought I might have a bit of luck and find you together here."

Muriel said: "I'll ring for them to bring you some dinner. I don't expect you've had any yet."

And as the inspector, who was known to neglect his meals very easily under pressure of his professional work, but to welcome opportunities of eating with equal readiness, made no denial, he was soon dealing with an omelette of the quality of which the Regent Street is inclined to boast, while he explained the unexpected result of the enquiries which he had made.

"As soon," he said, "as Gilson produced his birth certificate in the box, and gave other details of his early life, we started having them checked. It was just routine. We didn't expect he'd sworn anything false on such matters as that, but we like to know where we are.

"Well, as to that, you can't trip him up, for it's all true; but we found something that seemed startling at first, and may lead to an explanation of everything, but it's still hard to see how it can.

"The fact is that Gilson's got a twin brother."

The inspector paused for a moment, and Sir Reginald exclaimed: "The devil he has!" Muriel said: "I suppose we ought to have thought of that possibility;" and Mr. Jellipot, looking puzzled, said: "That is certainly an interesting fact, but I hardly see—"

"Neither did we," Combridge went on, "and we're further off now than we were at the start. But we saw we'd got to work fast if we were to have anything ready for you tomorrow morning, and—it was the superintendent's idea. I didn't like it, but it seemed to turn out well enough—I telephoned Gilson a couple of hours ago, and said we'd heard that he had a twin brother, and could he tell me his address, and what he's doing now.

"Gilson answered quite readily. He said he'd been expecting that question, and wondered it hadn't been asked sooner. His brother is a traveller in agricultural machinery. He represents Purley's, and he has been in Australia for the past three years.

"So he said; and when I'd got that I didn't lose any time. I rang up Lord Ratlin—he's the Chairman of Purley's—and he told me where I could get their secretary, and he told me that it's quite true. They've got a traveller named Gilson, and he's been in Australia and New Zealand for the past three years, and they hear from him every mail. He's a man in whom they have entire confidence, and he'd understood, though of course he couldn't swear to it as a fact, that it's his brother who carries on a stamp business in the Strand, of whom all London has heard in the last forty-eight hours. So that's that.

"It's a queer fact, but unless there were triplets instead of twins, I don't see how it's going to be of any use to us."

Mr. Jellipot said: "No, I don't see how it can be any use at all."

Sir Reginald said: "You may find, when you've raided Haslett Street, that it fits in somehow. You won't get far, if you ask me, till you've done that."

"We can't do that," the inspector replied definitely. "Not without a lot more reason than we've got now. I don't say it mayn't be different if you get something out tomorrow. But it wouldn't be any use asking for a search warrant on anything we've got yet."

Mr. Jellipot, who was most acutely aware of the thin ice on which he had selected to tread, said that there could be no doubt of that; and shortly afterwards the little party broke up, its elder members going their several ways; and if Reggie Tudor stayed on, and he and Belle forgot that she was a potential convict while they talked on more intimate matters, it was surely their business, rather than ours.

CHAPTER LII.

AN UNEXPECTED EVENT

BELLE went in her sister's company to the court next morning, conscious of more anxiety than she had felt at any time during the two previous days, for which it might be thought that she had rather less cause than before. But she saw that she approached an uncertain crisis, and had become aware the night before that even Mr. Jellipot, on whom she so greatly depended, was feeling his way forward with less than his usual cautious confidence. She remembered that she had heard him say on an earlier day that the mystery was too much for him.

She talked critically on the way concerning the cleanliness of the dock which was becoming her familiar abode, and wondered what Sir Charles Rentoul would say if he should find her scrubbing it when he took his seat; but Muriel was definite about the unwisdom of doing that.

So she had been to an earlier proposal, of an equally reasonable kind, that Belle should take a cushion for a seat which she did not find to be as comfortable as luxury might desire

Would it be contempt of court to do that? Possibly not, but Muriel was decided in her opinion that the experiment should not be tried.

So she entered the dock again, and became aware of a desert of empty seats between her and the reporters' table, which was as crowded as it had been on the previous days.

She saw that Evelyn had come, but Sir Reginald was not at her side. He had gone to his Kilburn branch, to instruct his subpoenaed manager on the attitude he should take regarding the information which he might be asked to give.

Gilson was not in his place, nor was Plumer, nor Bulfit. Mr. Jellipot was absent, and Berwick Law. Doubtless the legal gentlemen were consulting together till the last moment, in greater privacy than the court could give.

Inspector Combridge was not there. But there might be the same explanation. Probably they might all come in together.

Reggie was there, and he took the opportunity to speak to her in the freedom that there will be during the moments before a magistrate takes his seat, "Suppose nobody comes," she said.

"How soon could we all go home? Or should we have to sit waiting all day?"

Reggie's legal studies did not enable him to answer this with precision, but he thought correctly that the situation would not occur.

Still, Sir Charles took his seat, and the absentees had not arrived. He looked round with surprise, which hardly lessened as Berwick Law hurried in, followed by the defending solicitor.

Sir Charles glanced at the clock, and then at his own watch. Had he mistaken the time? But Bulfit now appeared, with his clerk, and Plumer, and Plumer's clerk close at his heels, and the arena was filling again.

"You will probably desire to conclude your cross-examination of the prosecutor, Mr. Law?" the magistrate asked.

Mr. Law said he would prefer to postpone it.

Mr. Bulfit rose to protest.

Sir Charles said: "Before I decide that, there are one or two questions I should like to ask your client myself. I think he had better be recalled now."

But Mr. Gilson was not there.

Mr. Bulfit proposed an explanation. He reminded the magistrate that he had directed the prosecutor to bring to court the correspondence and accounts relating to his transactions with Mr. Burton. That would necessitate a visit to his office, and he may have found that it had taken him rather longer than he anticipated to get the books and papers together.

Sir Charles paused a moment, and then said: "Very well, I expect he will soon be here." He was not sure that he had done right to give such a direction at all on the evidence which he had yet heard, and he was therefore slower to reflect on an absence which might have such excuse. He added: "Perhaps, Mr. Law, you will go on with your other witnesses."

Mr. Law called Chief Inspector Combridge, but again there was no response.

"Did he expect," the magistrate asked, in some surprise, "that you would be calling him this morning?"

Yes. Mr. Berwick Law was quite sure of that.

"Chief Inspector Combridge," Sir Charles said with continued patience, "is not one who would be likely to treat the court with any lack of respect. He will probably have a sufficient reason for whatever may have caused the delay. You have other witnesses, Mr. Law?"

Mr. Law said he had, but they had not yet arrived.

Sir Charles still took the delay patiently. "We will wait ten minutes, if necessary," he said. "Any moment, one of them may be here."

The court sat in uneasy silence. Belle wondered curiously what would happen if none of the witnesses should arrive within the allotted time.

But the question did not arise. There was still three minutes to go when Sir Reginald Crowe entered the court with the manager of his Kilburn branch, and a clerk behind them, bringing the records which the subpoena required.

Mr. Berwick Law, breathing a sigh of relief from a tension which would have been greater for him had not the prosecutor been one of the absentees, was about to put Mr. Bailey-Wren into the box when he observed that the attention both of the magistrate and the magistrate's clerk were concentrated upon a note which the usher had just handed in.

Sir Charles said, with an unusual gravity in his voice: "I have just had a telephone message from Scotland Yard. It appears that Chief Inspector Combridge is already on his way here. I think it will be well to defer the calling of other witnesses till we have heard what he has to say."

The court became silent again. It was evident that there must have been more in that telephone message than a mere intimation that the inspector was on his way to the court. But what could it be?

Sir Charles was leaning over to speak to his clerk again, but their voices were so low that even the reporters, immediately below them, could not hear what was said.

Now Inspector Combridge had arrived. He went into the box at once. He said: "Information has been received that Mr. Henry Gilson was knocked down by a bus in the Strand about an hour ago, and received injuries from which he has since died."

Sir Charles asked: "It was an accident, so far as your present information goes?"

"A constable who witnessed it says that it appeared to be accidental. Mr. Gilson was hurrying across the street to catch a bus, evidently on his way here, when he was knocked down by one coming from the opposite direction. He had with him a portfolio containing papers which he had been directed to bring to the court."

Berwick Law rose: "I apply for the defendant to be discharged."

Sir Charles said: "Yes...the case is dismissed." His voice gave no indication of what he thought.

Berwick Law said hopefully: "There will be the usual order regarding costs?"

Mr. Bulfit was instantly on his feet: "I must most strenuously protest—"

Sir Charles had evidently made up his mind on that matter also. He said: "I shall make no order for costs today. I will appoint a date on which either of you can apply."

Neither fully content, they gave way. It was an easy guess that Sir Charles had deferred his decision until he should know what the inquest verdict would be.

CHAPTER LIII.

Truth in a Far Land

MR. JELLIPOT said: "I heard this morning that I had to congratulate Reggie—may I say that I congratulate you both?—on an engagement which has not been an entire surprise."

"Yes, of course," Belle answered, with a smile which even Reggie might have been glad to have, "but it's no thanks to him. We shouldn't be engaged now if I hadn't told him that he'd got to ask me within ten minutes, or never see me again. Muriel said it was just what I ought to say."

"That," Mr. Jellipot replied, with a gravity of tone which his eyes denied, "must have been a source of satisfaction—and possibly of surprise—to you."

"It was a surprise all right. But Muriel knew it was the only possible thing to do. Reggie's got some silly idea about my having more money than he. And I always do say what I mean. I've mostly found it the best way."

"I wonder," Mr. Jellipot said reflectively, and then, with an inconsequence which was more apparent than real. "Sir Charles Rentoul has decided that he will make no order regarding costs. The verdict being what it was, it was clearly the fairest way."

This conversation took place in Mr. Jellipot's office about a fortnight after Henry Gilson's death, on which the coroner's jury had returned an open verdict.

It might seem that it had become a matter of no great importance that her costs should be paid out of the estate of the dead man, and, perhaps, no more than she was entitled to ask. But the magistrate had seen that it must have more than a monetary significance. To order that her costs should be paid from Gilson's estate would be going very near to deciding that the dead man was the murderer she had denounced him to be, and there had certainly been no evidence on which such a decision could be properly reached. On the other

199

hand, to have ruled that the defendant must pay the whole costs of the abortive action would have gone equally near to convicting her of the libel, and declaring his belief in the innocence of the dead man, of which he was unsure. So he left each party to the payment of their own costs, and the legal gentlemen, who recognized that the enigma was left unsolved, accepted the decision with no more than the formality of demur which they both felt that the occasion required.

"Yes," Mr. Jellipot repeated, "I am sorry that a substantial expense must fall upon you, but it is a matter on which I have never been entirely sure of what the truth may be, and it is clearly the fairest way."

To which Belle, with an infrequent use of Transatlantic slang, replied that that was "O.K." by her.

And while they spoke, a letter which Henry Gilson had written during the last night of his life to the twin brother, to whom he had confided all of evil or good that his life had known—a letter which would have explained that which they were never destined to know—was on its way to Sydney, in the hull of a liner that rolled on a beam sea, with Cape St. Vincent rising forward through the mist on its port bow:

Dear Edward,

If the Sydney newspapers are as enterprising as usual, you will have heard of the brutal murder that Ames committed, and almost certainly of my own death, long before you can get this; and though you will be sorry, I know you won't be altogether surprised.

The fact is, that I couldn't get rid of Ames, as, you know, for years past, I have been longing to do.

Of course, I have a share of responsibility for what happened, and the law, in its unimaginative way, would say simply that I am Ames, and that I deserve anything due to him.

It's only partly true, as you, at least, will find it easy to understand.

In fact, as far as I was ever able to reconcile myself to Ames' murderous plans—which I never thought he would put into action, as, at last, in a moment of evil impulse (and exceptional opportunity owing to an appointment I had in a nearby road) you will have learnt that he did—was that he would be obliged to disappear, and that I should never be vexed by his filthy habits or ashamed of his doings again.

So it worked, up to a point, well enough. But the trouble was that *he wouldn't entirely go.* After I had been Ames for several years for nearly half my time, I found it extraordinarily difficult to be myself for twenty-four hours a day, without some moments when the temptation to sink into the Ames ways would be more than I could withstand.

I meant at first to give up the stamps, and to devote all my time and money to the Kilburn business, which both Ames and I had really liked. But then I found that I *must* keep on the stamp business, and be myself *in my old surroundings* for some hours every day, or there would have been a real danger that I should become Ames in time, and that it would be Gilson who had gone.

And then I found I had left that too late, and I sold out of the Kilburn business entirely. That would have made me safe, in spite of a hysterical girl and one of the most persistent lawyers (a very decent fellow) you ever met, but for that habit of mixing up with women of which Ames was never able to break himself entirely, and which I had warned him constantly would be his ruin, if he wouldn't have sense enough to leave them alone.

I think I could beat them even now, and perhaps I shall; but it's more likely that I shall throw in my hand tomorrow, and after we've been so close together all our lives I can't risk not letting you know.

If I post this in the morning, it will mean that I've decided to beat them in my own way, and, if so, I shall also post you a parcel of my best stamps, which will be insured for £3,000, and the documents will be enclosed with this letter.

There'll be about £7,000 coming to you, apart from that, so if they try to settle up the estate for much less it may be worth your while to come home, and look into things here.

There's nothing worth talking about left in the name of Ames. He's *dead.* And how I wish I'd finished him off a few months earlier, as you know I was often threatening to do!

Am I sorry for it all? I'm not sure, even now.

You know that the idea came to me first because of my identity—it was scarcely less than that when we were young—with yourself. I wanted something quite different, which I meant at first should be really me.

I took a lot of pleasure in the elaborate way in which I had worked it out, with such details, particularly as to the old aunt, which most men might not have tried, and you can't say it wasn't successfully done.

But it wasn't a real success, for all that. It couldn't be a mere matter of wearing a wig, or being a few inches more round the waist. Ames had to *be* different, if it were to be such a disguise as no one could detect. And so, just because I am precise, Ames had to be slovenly. And because I am fastidious, Ames had to be coarse. And so on throughout. And, of course, it was possible to me, because there's something of everything in all of us—something of all that's bad, and of all that's good. And, of course, as a result, I got to hate Ames, and he hated me. And yet we worked together in lots of ways. We couldn't help that. We were worlds apart, and yet closer than any Siamese twins.

When I began this letter, I wasn't sure what I may be going to do tomorrow, and as I write I become more uncertain rather than less. I still think I could give them such a run that I should get away in the end. But it's the idea of being called Ames, perhaps being tried—even convicted as Ames. Think of that! It's a bigger risk than a decent man can be expected to take. And *it isn't true*. I hated Ames. If I'd known that he'd have given way to that sudden temptation and murdered Briggs—if I'd known it the day before, I'd have strangled him with my own hands.

Of course, I couldn't have done that. That's absurd. I'm not mad. But you, at least, will understand how I feel.

Yes, I think I shall choose the cleaner and safer way. But I shall have to do it so that they can't say that it's an admission that I'm really Ames. They must never know. It would be a disgrace that even in my grave I could not endure.

I can tell no one but you, and I know that there is no one else—not even Stella—what a pity we couldn't both marry her instead of tossing up, as we had to do—not even Stella—I might say especially Stella—will ever know.